James Patterson's
BOOKSHOTS

Flames

Sacking the Quarterback

New York Times Bestseller
Samantha Towle

$4.99 US / $5.99 CAN

ISBN 978-0-316-27658-0

9 780316 276580

5 0 4 9 9

EAN

James Patterson's

BOOK**SHOTS**
Flames

AVAILABLE NOW!

LEARNING TO RIDE

City girl Madeline Harper never wanted to love a cowboy. But rodeo king Tanner Callen might change her mind…and win her heart.

THE McCULLAGH INN IN MAINE

Chelsea O'Kane escapes to Maine to build a new life—until she runs into Jeremy Holland, an old flame.…

SACKING THE QUARTERBACK

Attorney Melissa St. James wins every case. Now, when she's up against football superstar Grayson Knight, her heart is on the line, too.

THE MATING SEASON

Documentary ornithologist Sophie Castle is convinced that her heart belongs only to the birds—until she meets her gorgeous cameraman, Rigg Greensman.

BOOK**SHOTS**

CROSS KILL

Along Came a Spider killer Gary Soneji died years ago. But Alex Cross swears he sees Soneji gun down his partner. Is his greatest enemy back from the grave?

ZOO 2

Humans are evolving into a savage new species that could save civilization—or end it. James Patterson's *Zoo* was just the beginning.

THE TRIAL

An accused killer will do anything to disrupt his own trial, including a courtroom shocker that Lindsay Boxer and the Women's Murder Club will never see coming.

LITTLE BLACK DRESS

Can a little black dress change everything? What begins as one woman's fantasy is about to go too far.

LET'S PLAY MAKE-BELIEVE

Christy and Marty just met, and it's love at first sight. Or is it? One of them is playing a dangerous game—and only one will survive.

CHASE

A man falls to his death in an apparent accident.…But why does he have the fingerprints of another man who is already dead? Detective Michael Bennett is on the case.

HUNTED

Someone is luring men from the streets to play a mysterious, high-stakes game. Former Special Forces officer David Shelley goes undercover to shut it down—but will he win?

113 MINUTES

Molly Rourke's son has been murdered. Now she'll do whatever it takes to get justice. No one should underestimate a mother's love.…

UPCOMING ROMANCES

DAZZLING: THE DIAMOND TRILOGY, PART I

To support her artistic career, Siobhan Dempsey works at the elite Stone Room in New York City...never expecting to be swept away by Derick Miller.

RADIANT: THE DIAMOND TRILOGY, PART II

After an explosive breakup with her billionaire boyfriend, Siobhan moves to Detroit to pursue her art. But Derick isn't ready to give her up.

EXQUISITE: THE DIAMOND TRILOGY, PART III

Siobhan's artistic career is finally successful, and she's ready to start a life with her billionaire boyfriend, Derick. But their relationship has been a roller-coaster ride, and Derick may not want her after all....

BODYGUARD

Special Agent Abbie Whitmore has only one task: protect Congressman Jonathan Lassiter from a violent cartel's threats. Yet she's never had to do it while falling in love....

HOT WINTER NIGHTS

Allie Thatcher moved to Montana to start fresh as the head of the trauma center. And even though the days are cold, the nights are steamy...especially when she meets search-and-rescue leader Dex Belmont.

A WEDDING IN MAINE

Chelsea O'Kane is ready to marry Jeremy Holland in the inn they've built together—until the secrets of her past refuse to stay buried. And they could ruin *everything*.

UPCOMING THRILLERS
BOOK**SHOTS**

$10,000,000 MARRIAGE PROPOSAL

A mysterious billboard offering $10 million to get married intrigues three single women in LA. But who is Mr. Right...and is he the perfect match for the lucky winner?

FRENCH KISS

It's hard enough to move to a new city, but now everyone French detective Luc Moncrief cares about is being killed off. Welcome to New York.

KILLER CHEF

Caleb Rooney knows how to do two things: run a food truck and solve a murder. When people suddenly start dying of food-borne illnesses, the stakes are higher than ever....

THE CHRISTMAS MYSTERY

Two stolen paintings disappear from a Park Avenue murder scene— French detective Luc Moncrief is in for a merry Christmas.

BLACK & BLUE

Detective Harry Blue is determined to take down the serial killer who's abducted several women, but her mission leads to a shocking revelation.

SPREAD YOUR WINGS AND SOAR.

Rigg Greensman is on the worst assignment of his life: filming a documentary about birds with "hot mess" scientist and host, Sophie Castle. Rigg is used to the celebrity lifestyle, so he'd never be interested in down-to-earth Sophie. But he soon realizes she's got that sexy something that drives him wild…if only he can convince her to join him for the ride.

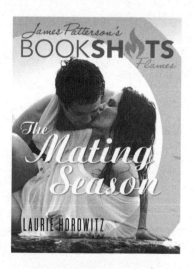

Read the heartwarming love story _The Mating Season_, available now from

Sacking the Quarterback

SAMANTHA TOWLE

FOREWORD BY

JAMES PATTERSON

James Patterson's
BOOK**SHOTS**
Flames

BookShots
Little, Brown and Company
New York Boston London

Copyright © 2016 by James Patterson

Hachette Book Group supports the right to free expression and the value of copyright. The purpose of copyright is to encourage writers and artists to produce the creative works that enrich our culture.

The scanning, uploading, and distribution of this book without permission is a theft of the author's intellectual property. If you would like permission to use material from the book (other than for review purposes), please contact permissions@hbgusa.com. Thank you for your support of the author's rights.

BookShots / Little, Brown and Company
Hachette Book Group
1290 Avenue of the Americas, New York, NY 10104
bookshots.com

First Edition: September 2016

BookShots is an imprint of Little, Brown and Company, a division of Hachette Book Group, Inc. The Little, Brown name and logo are trademarks of Hachette Book Group, Inc. The BookShots name and logo are trademarks of JBP Business, LLC.

The publisher is not responsible for websites (or their content) that are not owned by the publisher.

The Hachette Speakers Bureau provides a wide range of authors for speaking events. To find out more, go to hachettespeakersbureau.com or call (866) 376-6591.

ISBN 978-0-316-27658-0
LCCN 2016938303

10 9 8 7 6 5 4 3 2 1

RRD-C

Printed in the United States of America

FOREWORD

WHEN I FIRST had the idea for BookShots, I knew that I wanted to include romantic stories. The whole point of BookShots is to give people lightning-fast reads that completely capture them for just a couple hours in their day—so publishing romance felt right.

I have a lot of respect for romance authors. I took a stab at the genre when I wrote *Suzanne's Diary for Nicholas* and *Sundays at Tiffany's*. While I was happy with the results, I learned that the process of writing those stories required hard work and dedication.

That's why I wanted to pair up with the best romance authors for BookShots. I work with writers who know how to draw emotions out of their characters, all while catapulting their plots forward.

This is one of those books that's guaranteed to draw out your emotions. *Sacking the Quarterback* is a romance that is charged with sexual tension. Author Samantha Towle does a fantastic job of putting her character, Melissa St. James, in an impossible position—persecuting a famous football player who she not only believes to be innocent, but finds wildly attractive. And if you think that'll send you on a rollercoaster ride, just wait until Mel gives into her desires.

James Patterson

Sacking the Quarterback

Chapter 1

BUZZING.

Loud buzzing.

Something is vibrating close to my head. I force open an eye in my dark bedroom, which is now illuminated by the vibrating phone on my nightstand. Reaching out a tired hand, I retrieve my cell, catching a glimpse of the time as I do—*3:00 a.m.*—and see my boss's name lighting up the screen.

Benedict Cross, State Attorney. He became state attorney twenty years ago at the age of thirty-five, youngest ever in the history of Miami. He's a man I respect and admire greatly, and I want to be in the same position he is when I'm thirty-five, which means I have only four years left to make it.

Benedict isn't going anywhere, so if I want to achieve my goal, I'll have to move to a different city. And I'm completely fine with that. I have no ties here in Miami. My career is one of the reasons I keep myself attachment-free. And it's also the reason I'm working myself into an early grave, answering work calls at three in the morning. It's nothing new. I've always had to work hard to get everything. Nothing has ever come easy to me. And I prefer it that way. It makes success taste all the more sweet.

"Ben?" My voice is scratchy.

"Melissa, I'm sorry to call so late."

"Or early."

"Yeah," he says with a laugh. He knows I'm usually in the office by six thirty. "I need you to go down to the police station on 62nd Street."

It isn't out of the ordinary for Ben to ask me to go to a police station. Early-morning calls aren't strange either, but they don't usually come in at this time. Being a state attorney comes with its perks—the satisfaction of knowing that I put the bad guys behind bars—but these visits to the police station can be tough.

"Okay," I say, collecting my thoughts. "Who am I going to see?"

"Grayson Knight."

That makes me sit up and wake up a little more. "*The* Grayson Knight?"

"The one and only."

I'm surprised to hear the name. Grayson Knight, quarterback for the Miami Dolphins, is football's golden boy and everyone's favorite player, or at least everyone whose team isn't playing against him.

He's also seriously hot—not that it matters.

I run a hand through my tangled hair. "What's he done?"

"Drug possession."

My brows come up.

"He was arrested at Liv an hour ago."

Liv is an exclusive club at the Fontainebleau Miami Beach, a hotel the rich and famous frequent.

"Grayson Knight is high-profile, and men like him think they're above the law. We need to show him and the rest of the world that celebrities and sports stars are no different from anyone else who is caught with drugs. We need to make an example of him. I want you to go after Grayson with guns blazing. Getting a charge to stick to him won't be easy. It'll take my best. You're my best, Mel."

A burst of pride fills my chest at Ben's compliment. I know he thinks highly of me. I know I'm good at my job—no, I'm amazing at my job—but still, it's nice to hear it. And bringing down someone like Grayson Knight would be career-defining for me. It could be the case to push me up the career ladder sooner than I had hoped.

"I'll get down there now," I tell Ben.

"Call me when you're finished."

"Will do."

I hang up. Pushing back my duvet, I turn my bedside lamp on and put my feet on the floor. I take a quick deep breath and then head for the bathroom to get ready.

Thirty minutes later, I'm ready to go, briefcase in hand. I'm wearing a black business suit and a white silk blouse, but my face is free of makeup and my long chestnut-brown hair is tied back in a knot.

I'm not out to impress here. I'm here to do my job: get the lowdown on Grayson Knight before he lawyers up with some hotshot from a big firm.

Leaving my apartment, I take the elevator down to the lobby. Earl, the night doorman, is sitting at the desk. He smiles at me. "Early start, Miss St. James?"

"Too early." I smile back.

He chuckles. "Can I get you a car?"

"Don't worry, I'll flag a cab down outside."

"Let me do that." He gets up from his seat, coming around the desk.

I follow him to the front door of the building.

"Young girl like you doesn't want to be out on the streets at night alone. You never know what kind of crazy is out there."

The crazy that I fight against every day. The crazy that I'm trying to put behind bars to make the streets of Miami safer for other young women.

I don't say that out loud, though.

I love being an assistant state attorney. There's nothing better than putting away criminals and seeing justice served to up-their-own-ass jocks like Grayson Knight who think that just because they have money and fame, they're untouchable. Yeah, well, I'll show him just how touchable he is.

How touchable his body is.

I banish the thought from my mind. He is my opponent.

Earl flags down a cab. I thank him and climb into the backseat.

"62nd Street police station," I tell the driver as I sit back.

Chapter 2

I PAY THE DRIVER, tipping him well due to the hour, and get out of the cab. With my briefcase in one hand, I make my way up the steps to the doors of the police station. Pushing them open, I step inside to find the reception area reasonably quiet. That isn't strange at this hour. A man and a woman are sitting in the plastic seats off to my left. Cops are milling around in the office behind the desk. I don't recognize the on-duty officer. She's a dark-skinned woman in her midforties who looks far too alert.

I approach her with a smile, noting the name on her badge. "Hi, Officer Santiago, I'm Assistant State Attorney Melissa St. James. I'm here to see Grayson Knight."

She smiles at me. "He's being interviewed at the moment. Would you like me to take you through?"

"Please."

Officer Santiago comes out from behind the desk and I follow her through a door and down the corridor that leads to the interview rooms. She stops outside one of the doors. "They're in here."

"Thanks."

I knock once and open the door. Inside is Sergeant Matt Daughtry.

I dated him for four months and broke it off six months ago, even though he wanted it to continue. And he never makes any effort to hide that fact.

Jason Black, Matt's partner, is sitting next to him. I really don't like that guy. Something about him has always set me on edge, and I'm not feeling any differently about him right now.

Sitting across from them, with his back to me, is Grayson Knight.

Matt's eyes connect with mine. I tip my head back, indicating that I want to have a word with him outside.

"I'll just be a minute," Matt tells Jason.

All the while, Grayson, being the arrogant ass I imagine him to be, doesn't even turn to look at me.

Matt pushes up from his seat and comes out to me. The door closes. I move down the hall and lean my shoulder against the wall. "Melissa," Matt says, greeting me with my first name.

"Sergeant," I say, to remind him of what we are to each other now.

"You can call me Matt."

"And you can call me Assistant State Attorney St. James."

Laughing lightly, he shakes his head. "Is that really where we're at now?"

"Where 'we're at' is at work," I say, folding my arms over

my chest. "Fill me in on the night's events." I lift my chin again, this time in the direction of the door, the one Grayson Knight is sitting behind.

"We received an anonymous tip that someone had drugs on the club premises. Sergeant Black and I went down there with a few other policemen. We did a sweep and search. Grayson Knight was found with a large quantity of Schedule II drugs on him."

"Large?"

"Enough to make every person in that club high and happy."

My brow furrows. "He was the only one carrying?"

"We found some other small quantities on others there. Nothing substantial."

"Do you think it's strange that he was carrying so much? It's not like he needs to deal for the money."

Matt leans his shoulder against the wall, facing me. "Who knows why these celebs do what they do. Probably doing it for the kick."

"Hmm…yeah." My eyes go back to the closed door. "You were interviewing him without representation."

"He waived his rights. Said he doesn't want a lawyer."

I look back at him. "He doesn't want a lawyer? I guess that'll make my job easy."

"Yup. He said he didn't." Matt shakes his head.

Interesting. And unusual. The first thing celebrities usually do is scream for their attorney.

"You wanna talk to him?"

"Yeah. Give me a few minutes alone with him. Ben wants to throw the book at him."

Matt smiles, then pushes off the wall and opens the door. I walk through it. Jason gets up from his seat and, after brushing past me, leaves. I wait for the door to close before I take a seat in front of Grayson Knight.

He lifts his head slowly. My eyes meet the tired but striking green eyes of Grayson Knight.

Wow. Okay.

I'm a professional and I've dealt with celebrities before, but Grayson Knight is in a league of his own. It's hard not to be a little affected. I know football players are big guys. But Grayson is huge. Big shoulders, all muscle. And he's even more attractive than he is on TV. He exudes confidence and power, even in the tired state he's in. It's easy to see why America loves him.

But I'm not here to adore him. I'm here to stick him with a big fine or put him in jail. So I don my work armor and say, "My name is Melissa St. James. I'm the assistant state attorney on your case."

Chapter 3

GRAYSON STARES AT ME and doesn't say anything.

"Can you run through the night's events for me?"

"I already told the officers," Grayson says. His tone is almost bored, bordering on condescending.

Leaning forward, I rest my forearms on the table between us. "And now I want you to tell me."

He sighs. "I was in Liv. I had some coke on me for recreational use. The cops raided the club. They found the coke. They arrested me and brought me here. End of story."

"You're telling me the amount of drugs you were carrying was just for...recreational use?"

"I'm a big guy. What can I say?" He lifts one of those aforementioned giant shoulders.

When I look at Grayson, I immediately know the guy doesn't have a drug habit. I've seen enough addicts in my career to know the signs. This guy looks as clean as they come. Besides, if he was addicted to drugs, it would have been flagged in one of the many tests they do in the NFL these days. His team might have covered it up, but they also wouldn't have a high tolerance for him if he was a user. Addicts are generally unreliable and unpredictable. Grayson's contract wouldn't have been renewed, or his team would have found a way to get out of it.

Grayson Knight is their star player. And he was found with drugs. None of this is making sense to me right now.

But I don't need it to make sense. He broke the law. I'm here to see that he goes away for it.

"You waived your right to an attorney."

"Yes."

"Why?"

"Because I don't need one."

"You might want to reconsider, Mr. Knight." I stand up and walk to the door. Before opening it, I turn back to him. "Your release papers are being drafted up."

His eyes widen. "I'm free to go?"

"For now. I want you in my office in the morning at ten thirty sharp for your plea bargain. That's where I'll explain the charges against you, and you'll tell us how you'd like to plead in court. And, Mr. Knight, bring a lawyer to that."

He stands and moves to the side of the table. "That's it?"

"For now."

Something flickers in his eyes. Then I watch as his gaze drags up my body until it rests on my face.

I feel a surprising but delightful chill run through my body.

"I expected more." His tone is low and cuts through me, putting me off-balance.

"More?" I ask. My head feels suddenly foggy.

"Yes," he says, taking a step toward me.

He's still staring at me. Something in me wants to step back, yet there's another part that's urging me to go a step closer.

He's intense. And there's a raw magnetism in him that's drawing me in. I guess that's what makes him famous. That and the fact that he's an unbelievable football player.

There's a knock on the door behind me, bringing me back to my senses.

I give Grayson a hard stare. "There will be more. Because all actions have consequences, Mr. Knight. Irrespective of *who* you are." I yank open the door to see Matt on the other side and then look back at Grayson. Using a hard voice that means business, I say, "Sergeant Daughtry will sort out your release papers."

Since he's still standing there silently, I pull a business card from my briefcase and hand it to him. His fingers touch mine in the exchange. I steel myself against the jolt I feel. "My office details are on there. My office, 10:30 a.m. And don't be late." I turn on my heel and march out of there.

Chapter 4

GRAYSON HASN'T TURNED UP. It's 11:00 a.m., and he was supposed to be here a half hour ago. His lawyer is here—George Simpson, a man who works for the best law firm in Miami. No surprise there. Of course Grayson got the best lawyer in town.

At least he bothered to get an attorney. Shame he couldn't be bothered to show up for his plea bargaining.

Asshole.

"I can try calling my client again," George says, picking up his cell phone.

"No, it's fine."

It's not fine. I'm really pissed off. I don't like being stood up for anything. And I don't like when people make a mockery of me and my career. I get up from my chair.

George Simpson follows suit and stands. "How do you want to proceed?" he asks.

"I'll be in touch."

He nods and leaves my office.

I sit back down in my chair, my hands in fists. Who the hell does Grayson Knight think he is? *Asshole.*

But why am I really so pissed off by this?

Because I'm an assistant state attorney, for God's sake, and Grayson Knight thinks he can stand me up because he's what? A stupid football player. Well, guess what? I'm the law. He doesn't know what he's got coming.

Furious and unable to let this snub go, I make a quick call to Grayson's agent. I'm so angry that I let my emotions get the better of me and pretend to be his lawyer so that the agent will tell me where he is.

At a training session where his team practices.

The arrogant asshole went to practice instead of coming to his plea bargaining.

Armed with fury, I grab my bag and cell. I head out and catch a taxi on the street, telling the driver to take me to the Bubble, at Nova Southeastern University. That's where the agent directed me.

The taxi pulls up and I climb out. I make my way to the reception area, which is manned by a security guard. "Hi," I say. "My name is Melissa St. James. I'm here to see Grayson Knight. Harris Jones, Grayson's agent, said he would call ahead to let you know I was coming." Yes, I had pulled that little trick with Harris as well. Not my most ethical moment, but my anger is clouding my judgment, so I'm rolling with it.

"He did. I just need to see some I.D."

I pull my wallet from my bag and produce my driver's license. The security guard checks my I.D., then hands it back to me. I fill out the sign-in sheet and take the visitor's badge he hands me. I clip it to the lapel of my jacket.

"The team is training outside today on the main field. Take that door there," the security guard says, pointing. "And walk all the way down the hallway. There's another door to the field at the end, on your right."

"Thank you," I say, smiling at him.

I make my way through the corridor until finally I'm outside. The Miami Dolphins are on the field in the middle of a training session.

Now that I'm here, I'm not really sure what to do. It's not like I can just walk onto the field and interrupt the training session to demand to know why Grayson didn't turn up for our appointment this morning.

It takes me a minute to find him on the field, which is filled with big, sweaty men.

"Can I help you?" a male voice asks.

I turn around and see a guy in his midthirties who's wearing running shorts and a t-shirt. He has cropped blond hair and is attractive. But he's no Grayson Knight.

"Hi, I'm Melissa St. James. I'm Grayson's…attorney." There, I've lied again. "I have an appointment with him."

"Ellis Mitchell. I'm the team's conditioning coach," he tells me as he shakes my hand. "Grayson shouldn't be much longer. They're almost done here. Why don't you take a seat while you wait?" He gestures to the bleachers.

"No, I'm good, thanks," I say, giving him a polite smile.

"I should get back to it," he says, returning my smile. I have a feeling mine doesn't look nearly as warm as his. "Nice to meet you, Melissa."

"You too."

Ellis leaves and my eyes go to Grayson. In spite of myself, I can't deny that he looks really hot out there. And I don't mean hot in a sweaty way, even though he is. He's hot in the sexiest way imaginable. Grayson looks like the epitome of male out there as he throws the ball to his teammate. His jersey tight over his biceps, showing off the muscles in his arms. And don't even get me started on his legs. I'm pretty sure he could crack walnuts with those thighs.

Or me.

Jesus, where did that thought come from?

Of course Grayson is undeniably hot. But he's a criminal, and I'm intent on making a guilty charge stick to him like glue. A criminal who thinks he can ignore a plea bargain appointment with an assistant state attorney.

And he's a criminal who has just noticed I'm here. I see his head turn toward me, and I watch as he hands the ball off to his teammate before he starts to walk those powerful legs over to me.

And for some strange reason I feel a tremble in my own body.

Chapter 5

GRAYSON STANDS BEFORE ME with a frown on his face.

It makes me frown in return. Even though I'm angry at him, I can't help but notice his size and how hot he looks with sweat trickling down his neck.

"What are you doing here?" he says in a low voice.

What am I doing here? The nerve of this guy!

"You stood me up." I practically spit the words out.

All he does is raise a brow in return.

"Remember the plea bargain? To discuss your charges?"

Why am I so flustered right now?

He folds his arms over his chest. "I never said I would come."

I feel my eyes widen at first, so I narrow them quickly and say, "You don't get a choice in the matter. I tell you to come—you come."

He glances around at his teammates as they start to move in our direction. Then he takes hold of my elbow and starts steering me away.

I snatch my arm back. He opens the door I came through, giving me a look as if he's demanding I go through it. It makes me want to dig my heels in and stay where I am, but he's right. The field is not the place to have this conversation.

I follow him down the hall and stop behind him when he opens a door. I walk through it. He closes the door behind us and turns to face me. "What's the problem?"

"Seriously? You think I don't deserve your time. That you're such a big shot that you can just brush off your arrest. Do you think it'll all go away as if nothing ever happened?"

He takes a step toward me. "I don't think it'll all go away. I didn't turn up because I had to be at training, so I sent my lawyer in my place. The lawyer you told me to get."

"Funny. He seemed to think you'd be attending with him."

"Then he's an idiot."

"And you're the one who hired him. Wouldn't that make you an idiot, too?"

His lips turn up into a smile. I'd like to say it doesn't affect me, but it does. And I'd never let him see that.

"I told you to be at my office, Grayson. If I tell you to do something, you do it."

Something flashes in his eyes and he takes another step closer to me. The room suddenly feels a lot smaller. "I like a woman who takes charge."

"I don't care what you like in a woman."

He steps closer. "The thing is, I think you do care. That's

why you're so pissed that I didn't show up. That's why you've come all the way here...."

"You're very close to crossing a line," I tell him.

"Maybe I like crossing lines," he says, taking another step. He's close now. Too close.

My heart is beating hard in my chest. My breathing becomes quicker.

Take control of this situation now, Mel, before it gets out of hand.

Lifting my chin, I look him square in the eyes. "I came here," I say, "because you didn't show for an appointment"—*that's not exactly true; I came here because I was pissed off*—"and it was an important appointment at that. I was trying to do you a favor, but that was clearly a mistake. You can kiss the plea bargain good-bye. I'll see you in court, Mr. Knight."

Chapter 6

I PULL A BOTTLE of wine from the fridge and pour myself a glass. Carrying the wineglass and a large bag of chips over to the sofa with me, I put them down on the coffee table and turn the TV on.

After a long, shitty day and zero sleep, all thanks to Grayson Knight, I'm ready to relax for an hour before I hit the hay. With my remote in hand, I channel-hop while sipping my wine. I settle on a rerun of *Friends*. It's exactly what I need right now—some light humor.

I'm still chewing over Grayson's behavior earlier. I can't believe he was hitting on me like that. And I'm still trying to ignore the fact that it affected me.

That he affects me.

I stretch my legs out and rest my feet on the coffee table. My phone starts to ring. I reach over and pick it up from the table. The call comes up as a private account, and for a moment I consider ignoring it, but then I decide to answer. It could be a client. Always the lawyer.

"Hello?"

"Melissa?"

"Yes."

"Melissa, it's…Grayson. Grayson Knight."

Why the hell is Grayson Knight calling me at 9:00 p.m.? Actually, why the hell is he calling me, period?

Whatever his reason, I'm not going to make it easy for him. "How did you get my home number?" I ask. My tone is accusing.

"I, um…if I tell you, will you have me arrested?"

"Probably."

He laughs, but I'm not entirely kidding about having him arrested. I won't put him behind bars for this call, but it's my job to put him there for drug possession.

There's a distinct pause. I feel the tone in the conversation shift to serious as he blows out a long breath. "Can we…talk?"

"About?"

"Earlier."

I take a deep breath and let it out. Then I say, "You have one minute."

"One minute. Got it."

I hear him exhale loudly down the line. Again. But then he says nothing.

"Minute's ticking," I say, taking a sip of my wine.

"Right. Look, I'm calling to apologize for my behavior earlier. I acted like a total dick. Not showing up for our appointment, and for the way I behaved…I'm sorry."

"Okay."

"Okay…as in, okay, you forgive me?"

This guy is actually charming when he's not acting like a total tool. A smile is fighting its way onto my lips. I'm just glad he can't see it.

"Who helped you realize you were being a jerk?"

He laughs again, this time knowingly. "My dad might have chewed my ass out after my idiot lawyer told him that I hadn't shown up for our appointment."

There's another pause. Charming he may be, but I'm going to make this guy work for it.

"So…am I forgiven?"

"Maybe."

"Maybe. Okay. I'll take that," he says, chuckling softly. "And now this is the part where I ask you to keep that maybe-forgiven part in mind, and agree to meet with me tomorrow to discuss that plea bargain you wanted to talk about this morning."

I sit up, put my glass on the coffee table, and say, "I don't know."

"Please." When he says the word, there's a plea to his tone, and that starts to weaken my resolve. "I won't screw around. I'll be there whatever time you say. I swear."

I pause, thinking. I can hear him breathing.

Ben wanted me to throw the book at him, but I have this nagging feeling that I don't know the whole story here. And the lawyer in me has to know what it is.

"Okay, be at my office at 10:00 a.m. tomorrow morning."

"I'll be there. Thank you, Melissa."

"You're welcome. And, Grayson?"

"Yes?"

"This is your last chance. Don't screw it up."

Chapter 7

"GRAYSON KNIGHT IS HERE to see you," my assistant, Jill, says over the intercom.

I press down on the button and say, "Send him in."

I grab Grayson's case file and my notepad and pen and take them with me to the small meeting table I have in my office. Putting the file on the table, I take a seat on the chair that faces the door.

When the door opens, revealing Grayson, I have to hold in a breath to stop from gasping.

Holy shit, he looks amazing.

He's incredibly handsome. Like, out-of-this-world handsome. He's wearing a closely fitted black suit. And as I take in his size, I assume that it must have been tailored to fit him like that.

"Hey," he says, smiling at me. His teeth are dazzling.

I force my brain to function. "Hi. Great. Uh, take a seat," I say, gesturing to the chair across from me.

"Can I get you anything to drink?" I ask as he sits. This gives me time to compose myself.

"Water would be good."

I go over to the mini-fridge I keep in my office and grab two bottles of water. "Bottle okay, or would you like a glass?"

"Bottle's fine," he says, giving me another smile.

Jesus, stop smiling at me. And stop looking so damn hot.

I hand him his water and take my seat. Grayson unscrews the cap and takes a drink. I can't help but watch as he swallows that water down. The way his strong neck works on the movement. He lowers the bottle from his lips, catching me staring. Then his tongue darts out to catch the drops of water on his lips.

Holy mother of God.

That tongue…I wonder how it would feel to have his tongue on my…

I press my thighs together.

Stop it, Mel.

I force myself to look away and down at my file.

"Let's discuss the events that led to your arrest on the night that you were at Liv." I open my file to the police report detailing the arrest and pick up my pen, ready to take notes.

Grayson still has the bottle of water in his hand. He screws the cap back on and leans back in his seat. "I'd had a hard day training," he says, "so I went out with some buddies to let off steam. We ended up in Liv. We were drinking and having a good time. Then the cops showed up. I was searched and they found the drugs on me, and then I was arrested."

"Okay, let's start with the first part of the night. You say you went out—to some bars?"

"Yes."

"Which ones?"

"Can't remember."

"Where did you get the drugs? Did you already have them before you left home, or did you buy them while you were out?"

"While I was out."

I make note of that. "Which bar did you buy the drugs in?"

"I don't know."

"You don't know?" I ask, looking up at him.

"I don't remember," he says. His hand curls around the water bottle.

"Who did you buy the drugs from?"

He gives me a look and says, "A dealer."

"And his or her name is…?"

"I don't know," Grayson says again, unscrewing the cap of his water bottle and taking another drink.

I watch him again with my attorney eyes and see how uncomfortable he looks right now. I know he's at least looking at a big fine and all the negative publicity that goes with it, but there's something else going on here. Something he's not saying.

It isn't my job to save Grayson from a guilty charge—it's my job to give it to him. But I'm also not someone who will charge blindly. More than that, I like to know all the facts before I try someone. And I feel like I don't know all the facts here. Grayson's clearly hiding something.

"So, you're telling me you don't know the name of the person you bought that large quantity of drugs from?"

He lowers the bottle to the table, looks me in the eye, and says, "I told you, I don't know. He was some guy in the club that I bought drugs from. End of story."

"But you said you bought the drugs from a dealer in a bar, not the club."

"Club, bar. They're the same thing."

"No, they're not."

"Whatever. Jesus. Look," he says, leaning forward, resting his forearms on the table. He stares me in the eye as if that will make me back off. "I was in a bar. I went up to the guy because I knew he was a dealer—"

"How did you know he was a dealer?"

"Because I just knew."

"How?"

"Because he looked like a dealer."

"He looked like a dealer? How do dealers look?"

"Jesus! I don't know!" He's getting flustered. And he'd only be flustered right now if he were lying.

"But you just said you did. You said he looked like a dealer."

He clenches his jaw, and a frustrated breath leaves him.

"Grayson, I can't help you if you aren't truthful with me."

His eyes flash to mine. "I thought it was your job to put me inside—not to help me," he says, and I have to admit that he has a point.

So why do I feel the incessant need to do it?

"You're right. And based on what you're telling me, there's no plea deal that I can offer you."

"So we're done here?" he says without meeting my eyes.

I put my pen down, sigh, and say, "Yes. We're done."

Grayson stands. I feel a weird pull at the thought of him leaving right now. Once he reaches the door, he stops and looks back at me over his shoulder. "Thank you for your time. See you, Mel."

His words and stare hit me in the gut. And then Grayson Knight is gone, my door closing softly behind him.

Chapter 8

"PASS THE SALT," Tori says to me.

"Who puts salt on pasta al forno?" I say, frowning.

"I do," she says, giving me a cocky smile. "Now pass it over."

Tori is my best friend. I met her at law school. She works at a private practice, specializing in family law. Honestly, I don't know how she does it, dealing with people getting divorced, fighting the custody battles.

As a child of divorced parents who hated each other and fought over who got to see me the most, I've had my fair share of that pain. No way would I want to deal with it on a daily basis like she does.

Give me criminals any day. But I'm not really sure what that says about me.

I hand the salt to her and say teasingly, "Does my cooking not taste good enough for you?"

I had made dinner, and though I'm not the best cook, I can rustle up some decent al forno. Tori and I make sure to have dinner together at least once a week. Tonight we were supposed to go out, but I didn't much feel like being social, so I changed our plans and said that I would cook.

"It tasted just fine," she says with a grin, bringing a forkful of some salt-covered pasta to her mouth. "But now it tastes even better."

Picking up my wineglass, I give her a sly middle finger, grinning as I do.

"So classy," she says, laughing.

"I learned from the best."

Then it's her turn to flip me off, causing us both to laugh. And it feels good to laugh, after the past few days I've had. After the laughter has settled, I tuck back into my pasta.

"So why didn't you want to go out tonight?" Tori asks.

"Just didn't feel up to it," I say, lifting my shoulders.

"Work getting you down?"

"You could say that." I put my fork down on my plate.

"Wanna talk about it?" She forks more pasta into her mouth.

"No—" I pause. I can tell Tori anything. Anything within legal parameters, that is. "Yes."

She laughs.

"It's just this case I'm working on…I feel conflicted."

"Conflicted?" Her brows rise.

"I just…I think the guy is hiding something. I don't think the case is as clear-cut as everyone else thinks it is."

"You mean as clear-cut as Ben thinks it is."

"Yeah." I sigh.

"So, you think this guy is what? Innocent?"

I chew on my thumbnail. "Maybe not innocent. Just not as guilty as he appears."

She studies me for a minute, then says, "Go with your gut, Mel. You have great instincts. You think there's more to this, then find out what it is. What if Ben makes you put the guy in prison? You give jail time to an innocent man and find that out after the fact…I know you, it'll eat away at you forever."

Chapter 9

I'M JUST SHUTTING DOWN my computer when Ben comes into my office.

"Hey. Everything okay?"

"Yeah," he says, but he doesn't sit. He stands behind the chair on the other side of my desk, hands resting on the top of it. "I've just been reading over the Grayson Knight case."

"Okay," I say, waiting to hear what he's going to tell me. My heart starts to beat a little faster. I don't know why. "What do you think?"

"I think your proposal of charging him with possession of a Schedule II drug is too light. I was reading over the police report, and the amount of drugs he was carrying...I think we should push for possession with intent to supply."

"You do?"

"You don't?" he says, his brows pulling together.

"It's just...he's Grayson Knight. Superstar football player. Squeaky-clean record. Incredibly wealthy. Arguing for possession with the intent to supply will be a hard sell. It's not like he needs to deal drugs to make money. I think a judge would more likely accept a charge of possession of a Schedule II drug. That way, we still have a good chance of winning the case in front of the public."

"I disagree," Ben says, and his words are biting. I'm surprised, because Ben rarely disagrees with me, and when he does, he does it respectfully. "He won't get enough jail time with a Schedule II felony. With a good lawyer, he'll only get probation and a fine. Maybe community service. I told you that I want to make an example of Grayson Knight. That charge won't make an example of him."

"Okay," I say, unsure which tack to take right now. "So… you're saying you want me to…?" I let my words drift so he can fill them in.

"Up the charges to possession of a Schedule II drug with intent to supply. Let's make him look at a felony in the second degree."

I nod once in assent.

"Okay, then," Ben says. He pushes off the chair and takes a step away. "You're leaving for the night?"

"I was heading out, but I can stay. Do you want me to draw up the charges tonight?"

"No, go home. Do it in the morning."

"Okay."

"Good night, Mel."

"Night, Ben."

I watch him leave my office, my door closing behind him.

His words rattle around in my head.

Why is he so insistent on putting him in prison? I know that putting a high-profile celebrity like Grayson away would look good for him. But there are no elections till next year. And Ben is highly respected in Miami. It's not like he needs to pull tricks to get reelected.

Ben's words, mixed in with Tori's from last night, swirl around in my head.

What Tori said was right. If I prosecute Grayson without knowing the whole truth and he ends up going to jail as an innocent man, it'll eat away at me. Especially now, since Ben wants me to up the charge so that Grayson will be looking at some serious jail time.

I got into this job to do good. I want to be the best assistant state attorney, and to me, that means being honest. I don't want to put people in jail to better my numbers—I want to do it because those people deserve to be in jail. I want to do it to make my city a safer place—not just to get good publicity. And that's why I find myself dialing Grayson Knight's number.

He takes a while to answer the phone, and when he does, he sounds out of breath. "Mel," he huffs.

I love the way he calls me Mel. But my stomach sinks as thoughts flash through my mind as to what's causing Grayson to be out of breath. *Is he...with a woman?*

God, I hope not.

"I'm not interrupting anything, am I?"

"No. I'm just in my gym, working out."

"Oh." *Sweet relief.*

I shake away my thoughts. I want to get to the truth, not bone the guy.

"Is everything okay?" he asks.

"Yes…I was just wondering if you have time for a chat."

"Sure." He doesn't ask why. And honestly, I feel a flutter of content that he's so quick to answer yes. "Do you want me to come to your office?"

I don't think it's a good idea to meet Grayson here—Ben could find out about it. But there's a coffee shop I really like that's on the other side of town, not far from my apartment. And I never see anyone from work there. Grayson and I will be able to talk in peace.

"Can you meet me at the Hideout instead? It's a coffee shop on—"

"I know where it is," he interjects. "I love that place. What time did you want to meet?"

I glance at the clock. "How long will it take you to get there?"

"I just need to grab a quick shower. I'm all sweaty from the gym."

A nice image pops into my head. *Grayson is all sweaty, naked, and hovering over me as he…*

Stop it, Mel!

"It'll probably only take me ten to shower and change, and another ten to drive over."

I clear my throat, but when I speak, my words still come out ragged. "I'll see you in twenty, then."

"See you soon," he says, and hangs up.

I leave my office and head for the elevator. Downstairs, I flag a cab on the street.

The entire time, I desperately try not to think about the fact that Grayson is probably naked right now. Naked and wet, in the shower.

Holy God.

I need to wipe these images and thoughts from my mind so that I have a clear head when I see him. I'm meeting him to discuss his criminal charges, and all I want to do is take off his sweaty clothes.

Chapter 10

I'M THE FIRST to arrive at the Hideout, so I order myself a latte and take a seat in a booth at the back of the shop to give us privacy. It's a good table because I can still see the door when Grayson arrives.

I don't have to wait long—only a few minutes. From the doorway, Grayson scans the coffee shop. His eyes land on me and he smiles.

And I feel that smile deep inside me, curling my toes.

I try to shake the feeling off, but it's not easy when he's walking over to me, his eyes clearly fixed on mine. Okay, so I'll admit it now: I'm definitely attracted to Grayson Knight. But I'm also the assistant state attorney on the case, and my job is the most important thing to me.

I need to push this attraction down and ignore it.

"Hi," he says. "I'm gonna order a coffee. You want anything else?" He nods down at my latte.

"I'm good, thanks."

I watch as he walks over to the counter, orders his drink,

and pays for it. He comes back over empty-handed. "Waitress said she'll bring it over."

He sits down across from me and there's a moment of quiet. I curl my hands around my cup, unsure what to say. How to open the conversation. It's very unlike me.

"So, you wanted to talk?" Grayson says, his voice soft.

I lift my eyes to him. "My boss wants me to up the charge against you to possession of a Section II drug with intent to supply." I see a flicker of something in his eyes, but his expression doesn't change. The words hang between us as the waitress comes over and puts Grayson's coffee on the table in front of him.

He breaks his stare and looks at her. "Thank you," he says. His eyes scan the coffee shop after the waitress has left our table.

Finally, he looks back at me. "Okay," he says.

"Okay. That's all you have to say?"

"What do you want me to say? The State Attorney wants you to up the charge. He's your boss. I'm assuming you do as he says. So...okay. Thank you for telling me."

I stare at him, perplexed. "How can you be so calm about this?"

"Why do you care so much?" he fires back. His words almost knock me out of my seat.

But he's right—why do I care so much?

The question is almost like truth or dare.

I say the truth, I'm done for. I don't and he takes on the biggest dare of his life.

"Because…" I lift my shoulder as I drag out the word and play for time. "Maybe I think you're not telling me everything about what happened that night."

"Even if I wasn't, why would that matter to you?"

"Because I don't want to put innocent men in prison when I can do something to avoid it."

I watch his hand tighten around the cup. His eyes stare down into his drink.

"Tell me what happened that night in Liv," I say softly, coaxing him.

He doesn't speak for a long moment. When he lifts his eyes, I hope to see something in them. The truth, maybe. But what I see is nothing. His eyes are blank. "I told you what happened," he says. "I got the drugs from a dealer in a bar. Then I went to Liv and the cops busted the place. I was arrested. End of story."

He's hiding something. His expression might be blank, but the small shift he just made and the way his eyes darted to the left—both movements tell me differently. I had a hunch that that was the case in my office the other day. But here in the coffee shop, I can see it clearly. And I'm not willing to let it go this time.

"How long were you in Liv before the cops showed up?" I ask. I want to question him to see if I can learn anything new.

"An hour, maybe."

"And the search, how did it go down?"

"They came into the VIP area. We were one of the first to be searched."

"'We'?"

"My friends…and my brother."

Interesting. I didn't know he had a brother. I wonder if he looks like him.

"And you didn't think to try to dispose of the drugs at any point?" I ask. Of course I don't condone that type of thing, but I see it time and time again—dealers disposing of drugs before the arrest can be made. It's hard to make a charge stick if the drugs can't actually be found on the person. Especially in a public place like a nightclub.

I hold my stare and watch Grayson shake his head. I don't know how else to push this, even though I know there's something he's not saying.

So I shift the conversation elsewhere—to football. He relaxes immediately, and we spend the next hour drinking coffee and talking sports.

One could call it a date. But it's not. It's definitely not.

But I won't deny that I like talking to him. He's smart and fun, and charismatic. He's also nice to look at, which is always a bonus.

Once I get him relaxed, I try to swing the conversation back to the charge, but even then, he doesn't give me anything to work with. After a few hours, my second coffee cup is empty. "I should go," I tell him. "I've got an early start in the morning."

Drafting up his new charges.

I feel my mood drop down like a rock in water.

"Yeah," he says.

I note the flicker of disappointment in his eyes, and I wish it didn't, but it lifts my spirits a little.

Okay, a lot. And, yes, I know how screwed up this is. I'm about to charge this guy with possession of a Schedule II drug with intent to supply, and some people could say that I've just been on a date with him.

Not a date!

Shit.

We both stand and leave the coffee shop.

"I'll walk you to your car," he says when we're out on the sidewalk.

"I took a cab here," I tell him.

"Then I'll drive you home," he says.

And I don't argue.

Chapter 11

I FOLLOW GRAYSON over to a shiny black Range Rover. "Nice car," I say as he unlocks it.

"Thanks." He opens the passenger door and I climb inside. He shuts the door behind me and makes his way around to the driver's side.

I put my seat belt on as Grayson climbs in the car, buckles up, and starts the engine. He pulls out into traffic. I can't help but watch him drive. There's just something so incredibly sexy about watching a man like Grayson drive. Looking at his strong hands around the steering wheel has my mind wondering what his hands would feel like wrapped—

"So where am I going?" he asks, snapping me out of my reverie.

"What? Oh." Flustered, I fire off my address to him. Then we slip off into silence. It's not uncomfortable but definitely filled with tension on my part.

It doesn't take us long to reach my place. I can't deny that I'm disappointed that my time with him is over—until I see him in court, anyway. You know, since I'm trying to put him in prison and everything.

Grayson pulls into the parking lot to my building and kills the engine. The tension between us feels so much heavier now in the dark and silence. I'm very aware of the fact that we're alone.

"Thanks for the ride."

"Thanks for inviting me to coffee. Even if it was to deliver bad news," he says. He glances over at me and smiles.

"I'm sorry."

"Don't be. I was the one who made the decision to carry those drugs with me. I wasn't going to sell them. But I had them. A lot of them. I have to face the consequences for what I've done."

I shift in my seat, facing him. "See, you weren't going to sell them. So why did you have so much on you? It doesn't make sense to me."

He looks away, his hands curling around the steering wheel, gripping. "It…I…it doesn't have to make sense to you. It's just the way it is."

"But it doesn't have to be this way. If I knew the truth, I could maybe—"

"You're not my lawyer, Mel." He turns to me, his eyes blazing. "It's not your job to fix this. You're the one charging me. Why does this matter so much to you?"

"I told you why it matters," I say, keeping my voice even and low to show him that I mean every word. "I don't like to put innocent men in prison."

"I think it's more than that. Tell me," he demands.

"Tell you what?" I fire back. And we're inches apart now, eyes locked together.

"This."

His mouth slams down on mine.

Chapter 12

HE'S KISSING ME.

Oh, God, he's kissing me.

Heaven. And hell. It's the only way I can describe what's happening right now.

The feel of Grayson's lips against mine, his tongue in my mouth, his hands in my hair…heaven. But then there's the message in my brain, screaming at me that I shouldn't be doing this. I'm the assistant state attorney on his case. I'm going to be standing on the opposite side of the courtroom, across from this guy, as I charge him with a crime. This is so very wrong. It's hell.

Just one more second. I'll kiss him for one more second and then I'll stop.

Grayson groans into my mouth. It's a sound that can only be described as sweet ecstasy, and I nearly come right there on the spot.

Holy shit. I'm so screwed.

I don't want to stop. He tastes so damn good…*feels* so

damn good. His hands leave my hair, skimming down my shoulders, my arms, coming around my waist as he pulls me closer to him. My hands slide up his biceps, curling around the back of his neck. His tongue slides along my lower lip, then he sucks it into his mouth.

"You feel so damn good, Mel," he says, and his voice rumbles against my lips, before he captures them savagely in an even hotter kiss.

I'm going to lose my job.

"Stop." I press my hand into his chest, pushing myself back and away. "We have to stop."

"Why?"

"Because!" I throw my hands up in the air and move back to my seat. I grab my bag from the floor and put it in my lap as a barrier. "I'm the assistant state attorney on your case! And you're a drug dealer up on a charge, you realize. I could get fired from my job for this!"

"Hey, it's okay," he says, reaching for my arm.

I dodge his move. "No, it's not okay. I'm the one who's prosecuting you."

Grayson doesn't say anything. What can he say? It's the truth.

I'm in so much trouble.

"I have to go." I pull away from him, reaching for the handle.

"Mel. Wait," he says. His tone is imploring, but I can't stay. I have to go.

I jump out of the car and slam the door shut behind me. I hear him get out, too, and then he's calling my name, but I'm practically running to my building.

I'm relieved to find that the lobby is empty. I furiously press the button for the elevator. When it arrives a few seconds later, I practically fall into it. I lean back against the wall as the doors close in front of me and the elevator begins to ascend slowly.

Jesus Christ, what was I just thinking! Clearly I wasn't. Otherwise I wouldn't have been making out with the defendant in the front seat of his car.

I can't believe I did that. That's not me. I don't do reckless things like that. Especially not things that would put my job at risk.

I let myself into my apartment and drop my bag on the counter. Just as I do, my cell starts to ring. I go through my purse and pull it out.

Grayson's calling.

I stare at his name for a long moment. And for the first time in a really long time, tears well up in my eyes.

I reject his call, leave my cell on the kitchen counter, walk through to my bedroom, and undress. Falling into bed, I let the tears flow. *How did I make that mistake?*

But that's when I realize that my tears are about something else, too.

Because I can't have what I want.

And right now, that's Grayson.

Chapter 13

I'VE SHUT DOWN my computer. I need to talk to Ben. Though I've been putting this off all day, I can't put it off any longer. I want off this case. In all honesty, I also have to tell him that there's a personal conflict. I'll have to deal with the consequences, whatever they may be. My stomach roils with unease. Forcing strength, I get up from my desk and leave my office, heading down the hall.

Ben's door is ajar, and I hear him talking to someone. It takes me a moment to realize that he's on the phone. I'm just about to walk away when he says something that catches my attention.

"—Dolphins versus Browns, next month. Yeah, put fifty grand on the Browns." Silence, and then he laughs. "Yeah, well, maybe I've got a good feeling about this one."

Feeling sick, I take a step back, my hand pressed to my stomach. I glance around to make sure no one has seen me and hurry back to my office.

I close the door behind me and lean against it, feeling off-balance.

What the hell did I just hear?

Ben wouldn't be pushing up Grayson's charge just to win a bet, right?

Grayson is the star quarterback. If the team loses him, they'll probably lose most of their games. Even against a team playing as poorly as the Browns are this season.

Ben wouldn't do that.

Would he?

I slump down in my desk chair. My cell rings on my desk. I pick it up, answering on autopilot as I usually do during the workday, and don't even look at the caller display.

"Melissa St. James."

"Mel," Grayson says. His deep, masculine voice hits me square in the chest.

It takes me a moment to speak, and all I manage to say is: "Hi."

"Hey," he says.

There's a beat of silence between us. An unspoken word, filled with everything that happened between us last night.

I shut my eyes. But behind my lids, all I see is him. Kissing me. Touching me. Wanting me.

I can't do this. I open my eyes and say, "Why are you calling? Because if it's—"

"Wanted to hear your voice."

With that one utterance, Grayson knocks the wind out of my sails. I lose my resolve.

He wanted to hear my voice. I feel like crying in frustration. He's being so sweet and I want him so very badly.

And my boss is trying to put him in prison. Actually, he wants me to put him in prison. I'm royally screwed. I have no clue what to do. For the first time in my life, I don't have the answer to this. I really hate the universe sometimes.

"You shouldn't say things like that to me," I tell him.

"You think I shouldn't. I think I should. One thing you should know about me is that I always tell the truth. So I'll keep saying those things until you start listening to them. I want to hear your voice, I'll call you. I want to tell you that I want you, I will. And, Mel, I do want you. Whether you want to hear that or not, I'm still going to say it. It doesn't make it any less true."

Oh, God. Now he's being all forceful and alpha, and it's so goddamn hot. He's got me spinning in circles.

"Now, I'm going to tell you that I want to see you. That I *need* to see you." His voice is low and deep, almost a growl, making me shiver.

"That's…that wouldn't be a good idea," I say, because it's true. It would be the worst idea ever. But also probably the best idea.

It's only because he's forbidden, I tell myself. We all want what we can't have, right? It makes it all the more desirable.

Even as I think the words, I know they're not true.

I would want Grayson even if he was readily available to me.

There's just something about him…something that has gotten under my skin and embedded itself deep inside me.

"The best things usually come from the worst ideas," he says seductively.

"I…can't."

God, I want to punch myself in the face. *Just end the call. Get off the phone. Tell him no, and stop torturing yourself.*

But then his tone changes and he says, "I really do need to see you. Just to talk. About the case. Nothing else. I'll keep my hands to myself, I promise." His voice sounds soft and sweet. And just like that, all bets are off.

Because, goddamnit, I *want* to see him, too.

"Where are you?"

"I'm at the Bubble. Come in through the field entrance. I'll tell security to let you in."

"I'll be there in ten."

Chapter 14

I IGNORE THE TREMOR of excitement that I feel in my stomach as I walk toward the entrance of the Bubble, knowing that I'm going to see Grayson very soon.

When exactly did I turn into a fangirl for him?

Probably around the time he stuck his tongue in my mouth, making my body come alive for the first time in years.

Yep, that was the exact moment.

I can see that the main entrance is all closed up. The lights are out, but Grayson said that I should come in through the field entrance.

If only I knew where the field entrance was. I look around for a sign, see nothing, and decide to walk around until I find it. I'll give it ten minutes before I call Grayson and have him come get me.

I begin walking down the length of the Bubble. The area's well lit, so it isn't completely scary. But I am relieved when I round the side and see a guard standing by a door. He looks up at me.

"Hi," I say. "I'm here to see Grayson Knight. He's expecting me."

"Yeah, he said to let you in when you arrived," he says, and stands aside, opening the door he was guarding.

I step through and hear it clang shut behind me. And then I'm on the edge of the football field. Floodlights all the way around illuminating it.

And there's a solitary figure in the middle of the field, facing away from me.

Grayson.

I can tell that it's him from the line of his broad shoulders and the way he holds himself. Proudly, but like he's got the weight of the world sitting on him. His hand comes to his side and I can see a football in it.

I take a step onto the grass, and he turns to face me as if he's sensed my movement.

I can't see his expression because he's too far away. But I can definitely feel the heat and electricity that seems to connect us. It travels across the field and right into the very core of my body. And the pull is begging me to race in Grayson's direction, right into his arms. Or bed.

Crap. I'm so screwed.

On wobbly legs, I start to walk slowly toward him. *Thank God I wore flats today.*

Grayson doesn't make a move. He stands there, watching me walk to him. I feel like he's slowly undressing me with his eyes. It's torture. And it puts me on edge. God, I'm so nervous.

My stomach is rolling, and my heart is doing jumping jacks in my chest. I don't know what I'm going to say when I finally reach him.

All I do know is that Grayson makes me feel out of control. And I'm not used to being out of control. Control is what shapes me, keeps me moving forward in the safe life I've created for myself. Grayson seems to strip all of that away, leaving me vulnerable and bare. Yet I can't seem to stay away from him.

Finally I reach him. I stop a few feet away. "Hi," I say, my voice sounding small in the expanse.

"Hey." He flashes a smile at me, and I almost swoon.

Jesus Christ.

"Are we alone? Apart from the security guard." I tip my head in that direction.

Grayson puts the ball down on the ground by his feet. He takes a step toward me. "Yeah."

I step back. "We shouldn't be seen together. Not with the way things are at the moment."

He frowns, his brows drawing together. "So why come at all?"

I wrap my arms around my stomach, looking at my feet. I shift on the spot. "Because…"

"You wanted to see me."

I lift my eyes back to him. "I did. But I shouldn't. This—" I say, gesturing between us with my hand. "What happened last night. Can't happen again. I'm the assistant state—"

"I know," he snaps. "You've already told me a hundred times."

"I'm saying it because it's true."

He closes the space between us by reclaiming that step. "If things were different?"

"But they're not."

"If they were?" he asks, keeping his eyes firmly on me.

I hold my thoughts for a while, lips pressed together. "Grayson, I can't…"

Disappointment flashes through his eyes. He turns away from me. "I'm sorry that I kissed you last night," he says, and his voice is quiet and it breaks my heart. "I was out of line. It won't happen again."

"Okay," I say. What else can I say? I'm glad that he isn't looking at me right now, because I know that the disappointment that's lancing through me is showing on my face.

He turns back to me. His expression is fierce as he says, "When I say I'm sorry, Mel, I mean I'm sorry for the way I made you feel when I kissed you. The last thing I ever want to do is make things hard for you. But…" He takes a large step in my direction, his long legs eating up the space between us. He's so close now that I have to tilt my head back to look in his face. "*I'm* not sorry it happened. I'll never be sorry it happened. Because I wanted to kiss you. Goddamnit, did I want to kiss you." His eyes go to my lips. "I always want to kiss you. I have from the first moment I saw you."

He lifts his eyes from my mouth back to my eyes. My body starts to tremble.

Holy crap. I'm so screwed.

"I…" I part my lips to say something. What that is, I have no clue. So I close my mouth again.

Grayson pushes a hand through his hair. "I know you don't want things to be that way between us, so I'll back off. I just wanted you to know how I feel. Now that I have, I won't bring it up again."

My heart sinks so hard I'm pretty sure it's in my foot.

In my heart I'm screaming, *I do want to be with you!* That's the problem. I want him and I can't have him.

How do I tell him how I feel without actually telling him?

I rub my forehead with my fingertips, frustrated. I take a breath and say, "Grayson, my job is everything to me. *Everything.* I've worked really damn hard to get where I am today, and I'm still not where I want to be. I want to go further. I want to be state attorney someday. And I won't do anything that will risk that happening."

He leans down and picks his ball back up. Holding it between his large palms, he stares down at it while he says to me, "I get that, Mel. I do. I really wish I didn't, but I do understand." His eyes come back up to mine. "But I have to know. If things were different. If I wasn't up on this charge. And we were just who we are, and I kissed you—"

I cut him off. "If you weren't up on this charge then we wouldn't know each other. We don't exactly run in the same social circles."

"Stop evading and just answer the damn question."

My mouth goes dry. He knows the truth. He knows I'd be

with him in a heartbeat. I don't know why he's forcing me to say it.

Saying it out loud will do neither of us any good. It'll just remind us of the reason we can't be together. So I choose not to say it. I choose to remind him of why we can't be together.

"I'm the assistant state attorney who's prosecuting you, Grayson. Outside of that, nothing else matters. 'What ifs' and 'maybes' are pointless. What matters is the here and now, and that means that what happened last night will never happen again."

Chapter 15

GRAYSON'S FACE DARKENS. Anger and frustration and sadness all flicker through his eyes. It's a hell of a combination to see. His jaw is clenched tight and the muscles in his face work angrily. "I don't accept that," he says, and throws the ball to the ground. Just like that, my face is in his hands, his body is pressed against mine, and he's kissing me all over again.

This time I don't stop him. I couldn't if I wanted to. My body is weak to him. He kisses me with a passion and intensity that I've never before known.

Breaking from my mouth, he presses his forehead to mine. "How can you be sorry for kissing me when it feels like this?" he asks, brushing his lips over mine. "I want you. You want me. We can make this work."

I open my eyes. "How? Because I can't see a way we can work."

"Take yourself off the case. If you're not the one prosecuting me, then there's no problem."

"I can't do that," I say, shaking my head. I have to see his case through. And if what I overheard earlier is true, then Ben, my boss, whom I once admired, might be trying to set Grayson up for a big fall for his own gain. Financial and political. And if I'm not there, I don't know who will stop him.

"I'm the assistant state attorney," I tell Grayson, pretending that's the only reason. "I don't get to pass off cases."

Exhaling, he brushes his lips over mine and says, "I want this with you."

I wrap my hand over his wrist. "I know." *I want this, too.* "I don't see—"

"Don't say it." He cuts me off with his lips. "Just…don't say it."

I murmur my assent, letting him kiss me softly.

When we break apart, I take a small step away, needing space to try to clear my muddled thoughts. Grayson catches my hand, like he's afraid I'm going to run away.

I let my eyes drift over the field.

"Have you been training all day?" I ask, trying to lead us away from this thing that's happening between the two of us.

"Yeah. I've been out here all day, practicing. I love being on the field. Having a ball in my hand."

I understand that feeling. Except I love being in court, putting the bad guys away.

Pulling his hand from mine, he picks the ball back up from the ground and throws it clear across the field.

"Wow. I can see why they pay you the big bucks. You have a hell of an arm on you."

"Football is the only thing I was ever good at. If I can't play anymore…then I don't know what I'll do," he says, and there's a sadness in his tone that pulls at my heart.

"So why risk it all and take drugs to the club that night?" The words are out before I can stop them.

He doesn't look at me. Doesn't say anything. Just stands there, motionless. And even though my question was valid, I feel like a bitch. A little part of me feels like I'm using him— but of course I know I'm not.

I want to know what he's hiding, because nothing about him being caught with those drugs makes any sense to me. I want him to open up to me. Too bad the direct-attack tactic doesn't work with Grayson. I'm learning that very quickly.

I step up close behind him. "I could never throw a ball that far," I say softly. "I've watched you play in games and I don't know how you do that, get it all the way down the field with your accuracy."

"Years of practice. Hours spent on the field, in all weather." He picks up another football from the ground. "Here, I'll show you how to throw."

"Oh, I don't know." I take a step back. "I'll be terrible at it."

He chuckles low. The sound makes me smile. "You won't be terrible."

"I'll embarrass myself. I've never been good at sports."

"I'm going to teach you how to throw a football." He holds the ball out to me. No argument in his voice. It's a demand.

"Fine. But you'd better not laugh at me," I say, taking it from him.

"I won't laugh, I promise," he says as he comes to stand behind me. I'm aware of every inch of his nearness. My whole body is on alert. "Okay, so this is what you have to do to throw a perfect spiral."

"What's that?" I ask, glancing at him over my shoulder. He's a lot closer than I had realized. So close that I feel his breath on my cheek as he speaks.

"It's the type of pass the quarterback throws. The ball moves through the air, spinning like this," Grayson says, as he turns the ball in slow motion. "The whole game revolves around the perfect pass. This is it."

"Okay."

"So, hold the ball with a good, firm grip. Place the tips of your fingers on the laces. That's right," he says, guiding me. "You need a little gap between your hand and the ball." He moves it into position.

My breath catches at his touch.

"Perfect," he says. "Now lift the ball high on your chest. That's right. Relax your shoulders and let your arms hang loose." He presses his hands down on my shoulders.

Having him touch me like this, while standing so close to me…it's torture.

The best kind of torture.

"Okay, now put your feet shoulder-width apart. Good, that's right." He praises me as I move my feet into position.

"Now put seventy-five percent of your weight on the back foot."

"Seventy-five. That's very specific."

"I'm a specific kind of guy," he says, grinning.

I feel that grin like a soft caress between my thighs.

"Now," he says as his hands go to my hips, "as you move through your throw, shift your weight from the back of your foot to the front."

He rocks my body forward, demonstrating, and his hips press into my ass.

I feel something very significant prod me in the butt and I have to hold back a moan.

"You got that?"

"Mmm-hmm." I dare not speak because I'm afraid I'll say something I shouldn't.

He moves to my side. I almost sigh with relief. "Okay. Now," he says, "when you throw, you'll draw a circle with your elbow like this." He moves my arm, keeping his hand on my arm while he shows me. "Let the ball roll off each finger, starting with your pinky, so your wrist rotates. Your index finger should be the last thing to touch the ball as it leaves your hand. That's what generates the spin. Got it?"

"Got it," I say.

"Okay, so come back on your heels. That's it," he says, standing behind me. "Now, bring your weight forward, drawing that circle with your elbow, and then rotate your wrist as you throw."

The ball leaves my hand, going farther than I can normally make it go. It's even spinning, though it's a little bit wobbly. I admire my throw, but it's nowhere near as perfect as Grayson's was.

"I did it!" I shout as I turn to face him, beaming.

"You did good," he says. He reaches up and tucks a stray piece of my hair behind my ear. His fingers linger on my cheek.

I'm around 99 percent sure that he's going to kiss me again. And I really want him to. But then I hear the ringing of a phone.

Grayson lets out a frustrated sigh. He reaches into his pocket and pulls out his cell.

He frowns at the screen and then answers the call.

"Tyler…wait, what? Hold on. You're where? Jesus Christ, Tyler!" There's a sigh before Grayson says, "I'll be there in ten minutes. Yeah. Yeah. Just wait until I get there.

"Shit!" he curses, slamming his cell back in his pocket.

"What happened?" I ask, touching his arm to bring his attention to me.

"It was my brother, Tyler. He's been arrested," he says, meeting my eyes. "Drug possession."

Chapter 16

SUDDENLY THINGS START to make sense to me. I heard Grayson say those words and instantly knew, in no uncertain terms, that the man in front of me is in the position he's in because of his brother.

"I have to go to the police station," he says urgently, interrupting my thoughts. "I need to bail him out."

"That's not a good idea."

"Well, I can't just leave him there."

"I'm not saying you should leave him there. I'm just saying it's not a good idea for you—currently out on bail—to turn up at the police station to bail out your brother who has been arrested on a similar charge."

He steps back from me, thrusting his hands through his hair.

I want to tell him that I think I know what's been going on. That I know what he's been hiding from me. But I know that now isn't the time to confront him on that.

Later, I definitely will. Right now, I need to help him.

With a fire in my belly and adrenaline racing through my

veins, I take my cell out of my bag and dial Ben's number. Grayson opens his mouth to speak. I hold my finger up and stop him.

Ben answers on the third ring. "Mel."

"Ben, I'm just going to get straight to the point here—I want off the Grayson Knight case."

"That's not possible."

"I won't prosecute a man who I believe to be innocent." My eyes meet Grayson's. I see the flare of surprise in them. There's something else in them, too, something that makes my stomach flutter and tighten.

Ben laughs. "Grayson Knight is definitely not innocent. And you will continue with his case. If you don't, you're fired."

"You don't have to fire me. I resign," I say, and hang the phone up before he can respond.

I'm staring down at my phone when Grayson's hands touch mine. "Mel."

"Did I just quit my job?"

"It sounded that way." His voice is gentle, his grip on my hand tightening.

"Holy shit." I breathe out.

I just quit my job.

My job.

I love my job, and I just quit it.

"Are you okay?" Grayson asks.

I stare at him blankly. "No…I'm not sure. I think…I can't believe I just did that," I say, shaking my head.

"Not to seem like an insensitive asshole, but I have to go bail my brother out of jail."

That snaps me back to the present. To one of the reasons that I called Ben in the first place. Then I say, "I'll go to the station and get your brother out."

"Mel...I can't ask you to do that."

"You're not asking. I just know that it's not a good idea for you to be going to the police station right now. Not when you've been arrested for a similar charge. And honestly, Grayson, I think I know what's going on here."

He frowns at me and says, "I don't know what you mean."

"I mean, you're a guy who has never even had so much as a parking ticket. You have everything to lose if you face prison time for supplying drugs. Now your brother, who was there on the night you were arrested, is also sitting in a jail cell because he's been arrested for drug possession. It doesn't take a genius to figure it out."

His expression tightens. "You can throw whatever you think you've uncovered out the window, because you're wrong."

"Grayson—"

"You're wrong," he says with determination. "Whatever theory you've conjured up is wrong. And I don't need you to go get Tyler. I'll go bail him out myself."

Grayson turns to leave, but I touch his arm, stopping him. "Please...I'm on your side here. I quit my job because I'm that far on your side. I know you're holding something back from me. You don't have to tell me right now...but you should tell me, and soon. Now I'm going to help you by going to get your brother out of jail. Then maybe you'll believe that you can trust me."

He's staring at me like I've grown another head.

I step forward, closer to him. "Let me help."

"Okay." He softly breathes out the word. "Thank you…for everything." Then he leans close and presses a kiss to my cheek.

Chapter 17

I TAKE A CAB to the station. During the whole ride, my mind is working overtime. Why is Grayson taking the fall for his brother, who doesn't have as much to lose? Tyler doesn't have the media spotlight on him or the high-profile career that his brother has.

Sighing, I rest my head back against the seat. I really need to see Grayson's brother's rap sheet. If I can see that, then all my questions will probably be answered. I take my iPad out of my bag and log into the criminal database. I'm sure Ben hasn't gotten my access removed this quickly. I see that I'm right as my login works and I'm in straightaway.

I type in "Tyler Knight" and wait for the results to load.

My screen fills with enough information to tell me that everything I was thinking is correct.

Tyler Knight has a rap sheet dating back to juvy. But nothing as an adult.

From inside the system, I can see that he's been charged for small things like shoplifting, driving without a license, underage drinking, and criminal damage, but then for bigger things, like drug possession, as well. They were all things that Grayson could probably hide with his money. But if Tyler's caught with drugs as an adult, and with the intent to sell, then he'll be looking at serious jail time in an adult prison since he has a rap sheet like this.

But if his brother, the all-American football star, a guy who doesn't even have an unpaid parking ticket to his name, is found with the drugs on him, then we're looking at no jail time. A slap on the wrist, maybe a fine.

Until a crooked state attorney ups his charge to possession with intent to sell.

I call the station holding Tyler. It's the same one that had Grayson a few days ago.

"Hello, my name is Melissa St. James. I'm a…lawyer…and you're holding my client Tyler Knight."

So, he's my client now? Apparently so.

"Can you tell me if his bail has been set?" I ask.

"One second." I hear keys tapping on a keyboard. "Yes, bail has been set."

"I'll be there soon to pay it."

Chapter 18

MY LIFE HAS CHANGED a lot since I came here for Grayson's interview. I can't believe that was only a handful of days ago. I make my way inside, pushing open the door, and approach the desk. The officer on duty looks up at me. "Hi, I'm here to pay bail for Tyler Knight," I say.

"Sure thing."

"Can you tell me what he was charged with?"

The officer turns to the computer on the desk beside him, taps a few keys, and says, "He's charged with felony possession of the second degree. He was caught with a Schedule II drug with intent to sell." He glances back to me.

"How much is bail?"

The figure he tells me gives me pause. I mean, I am now unemployed. But I hand over my credit card and put up the money.

"He's in cell two at the moment," the officer tells me. "I'll call through and have him brought out to you."

I'm sitting on the waiting room seats, halfway through

a game of Candy Crush, when Matt Daughtry comes out through the door. He takes the seat next to me and I put my phone back in my bag. "You're here bailing out Grayson Knight's brother?" he asks.

"Yes."

"Do I even want to know why the assistant state attorney is bailing out the brother of the man she's currently prosecuting?"

I meet his eyes and say, "I'm not an assistant state attorney anymore."

I see the shock reverberate through him. "Since when?"

"About an hour ago."

"Jesus, Mel. What happened?"

"It's…complicated. I don't really want to talk about it right now."

He blows out a breath, staring ahead. "When I was told his lawyer was out here bailing him out, I thought they'd made a mistake when I saw you sitting here. So I guess…you're his lawyer now?"

I sigh and say, "I guess so."

I hear him exhale again, but I can't meet his eyes.

"Look," he says, placing his hands on my shoulder. "Just…be careful. I know Grayson Knight is a big celebrity, but…be careful, okay?"

I nod.

Matt stands, abruptly changing the conversation. "I'm having Knight processed. He'll be brought out to you soon."

"Thank you, Matt."

"Since you're his lawyer, you should know that his arraignment is set for two days from now. I don't consider him a flight risk, but he'll still need to turn in his passport tomorrow."

I know the process, but I nod my head and thank him again.

"Mel," he says, stepping close and lowering his voice. "I don't know what the hell has happened…but I do know how much your job means to you. You need someone to talk to, call me. Okay?"

"Okay."

Matt disappears back through the door he came through.

Fifteen minutes later, a disheveled, younger-looking version of Grayson Knight comes through the door. Matt is leading him forward with a tight grip on his arm.

"Thanks," I say to Matt, getting to my feet.

Tyler looks at me and then back to Matt. "Who's she?" he asks, jerking his chin in my direction.

"She's your bail money and ride home," Matt says to him, definite contempt in his voice.

I take a few steps toward Tyler and say, "I'm Melissa St. James. Your brother asked me to come and get you."

Tyler stares at me. "Why didn't he come himself?"

I glance at Matt and then back to Tyler. "He wanted to, but… it's…difficult, with his…situation. So I offered to come."

"You got this, Mel?" Matt says, heading for the door. "I need to get back to it."

"Yeah, we'll be fine from here. Thanks again, Matt."

Matt pins Tyler with a stare. "Remember I want you back here first thing tomorrow to turn in your passport."

"Yeah, yeah. I got it."

Matt gives a frustrated look and shakes his head. "I'll see you later, Mel," he says to me. Then he disappears behind the door, leaving me alone with Tyler.

"Well, thanks for coming to get me out," Tyler says as he heads for the exit. "Tell Grayson I'll call him."

"Tell him yourself."

He stops at the exit and turns to face me.

"You'll be seeing him soon. I'm taking you to his place."

"And if I don't want to go?"

"I'm not giving you a choice. You don't come with me, I'm taking you right back in there to Sergeant Daughtry and telling him I'm rescinding bail."

"You can't do that."

"I can do anything I want," I say, and put my hands on my hips. "So what's it going to be?"

He tilts his head to the side. "You're not like Grayson's other girlfriends."

"That's because I'm not his girlfriend."

Though I'm not really sure what I am right now.

"Fine," Tyler says as he walks out the door. I follow quickly after him. He's waiting near the side of the road for me. "You got a car, then?" he asks.

"No. We'll catch a cab to Grayson's place," I say. Then I stick out a hand to an approaching cab. It pulls over.

Tyler opens the back door and waves me in first. "I do have some manners," he says after I give him a surprised look.

The driver pulls up outside Grayson's house ten minutes later. Tyler and I haven't really spoken during the ride over. I thought it would be best to wait until he and Grayson were together before I started questioning them.

I find Grayson in his living room, standing by the fireplace, a tumbler of whiskey in his hand. A flash of relief passes over his face when he sees Tyler. But then the relief is gone and anger settles in.

"What the hell were you thinking?"

"Nice to see you too, bro," Tyler says as he throws himself down onto one of the plush couches. "You know, you look just like dad, standing there by the fire, glass in hand, pissed-off look on your face. I feel like I've just gone back ten years in time."

"Screw you," Grayson snaps, putting the glass down on the mantelpiece. He pushes his hands into his pockets and steps closer to Tyler. "How could you do this? You promised me that it wouldn't happen again."

"I didn't exactly have a choice," Tyler snaps.

"What do you mean you didn't have a choice? There's always a choice," Grayson says.

"Maybe in your perfect world there is. But in my world"— Tyler gets to his feet—"there isn't."

"I don't know how to help you anymore," Grayson says, sounding lost and frustrated.

"I never asked you to help me in the first place," Tyler says quietly.

"You're my little brother…I couldn't just…" Grayson's words die out and his eyes come to me. It's as if he's remembering I'm still here.

Tyler turns to look at me, too.

"Don't stop on my account." I wave a hand toward Grayson. "I mean, I think I've pretty much figured it out myself, anyway. Tyler has a history of criminal offenses. The cops raid the club. He has a sizable amount of drugs on him. Enough to put him away for a long time.

"Grayson, you tell him to give the drugs to you, so if they get found, neither of you will go to prison, because your record is clean and you're a notable figure in entertainment. You'll probably get a slap on the wrist—at the worst a fine and be put on probation. Only when it comes to laws about drugs, you don't know that Tyler was carrying enough to up the charge to possession with intent to sell.

"Because that's what you were doing, right, Tyler? You were going to sell the coke. Grayson took the drugs from you, got caught with them, and now he's looking at possible jail time. And I'm taking it the people you work for were not happy you lost those drugs that were seized from Grayson. Were they looking for their money back? Maybe you were out tonight, selling to try to make the money back to pay them off. Am I on the right track here?"

Tyler opens his mouth, but Grayson holds up a hand, cutting him off.

Grayson turns to me, his expression weary. He moves over to me, puts his hands on my arms, and says, "Mel...I need to talk to my brother...alone. I appreciate everything you've done for me and Tyler. But just give me tonight with him to talk."

Even though his voice is gentle, I feel stung by his words.

He wants me to leave.

"Trust me," he adds.

I step out of his hold.

"Sure," I say, as if everything is fine.

Chapter 19

I'M AT HOME, making myself some lunch, when my cell rings. I don't recognize the number but decide to answer it. Maybe I'm hoping it'll be Grayson, calling me from a different line. I haven't heard anything from him since he asked me to leave his house last night.

"Hello?"

"Is this Melissa?"

"Depends who's asking."

"Tyler—Tyler Knight."

"Oh," I say, surprised.

He pauses for a moment before he speaks. "I was just calling because…I wanted to say thank you for bailing me out last night."

"It's fine."

"Not many people would do that. You must care about my brother a lot."

"I…" I only get one word out because I don't really know how to answer that.

"I'm sorry about last night, with Grayson asking you to leave. He does appreciate everything you've done."

"Okay."

"He just...he thinks he's protecting me."

That gets my attention. "Protecting you from what?"

There's a pause on the line. "Can we meet? I don't want to talk over the phone."

"Does Grayson know you're calling me?" I ask. I don't want to go behind his back on this...whatever it is that Tyler wants to talk about. But then, if it helps Grayson, maybe he should be left in the dark.

"No, he doesn't know I'm calling. But I need help and there's no one else I can ask."

"You can ask Grayson, too. Talk to both him and me. Don't you think that the three of us should approach this together?"

"No. I...look, I'm just gonna come out and say it. I'm in trouble and Grayson...well, he's in trouble, too. But the thing is, he doesn't know it. I really need your help, Melissa."

"Okay," I say.

"You'll meet me?"

"There's a coffee shop on Ninth. I'll meet you there in twenty minutes."

"Thank you, Melissa."

I grab my purse and head for the door, my stomach twisting in knots. It's not that I don't trust Tyler or think he's out to hurt me. But he's definitely involved in something with some dangerous people.

I make a ten-minute trek to the coffee shop. I've been to this place a few times before with Tori. They do the most amazing carrot cake. And I could really do with some cake right now.

When I get there, Tyler hasn't arrived, so I take a seat near the window and order a coffee and a slice of my favorite dessert. The waitress brings over my order as Tyler pushes open the door. He looks harried and a little nervous. His eyes are darting everywhere. I lift a hand to get his attention. He spots me and comes over.

"Something to eat or drink?" the waitress asks Tyler.

"Just a black coffee," he says.

"Is coffee a good idea?" I joke.

"What do you mean?" he asks as his gaze darts to mine. He takes his jacket off and hangs it on the back of the chair.

"You look on edge. Like you've already had a bucket of caffeine."

"I need something hot."

We sit in silence until his coffee arrives. "Thanks," he says to the waitress when she puts it down in front of him.

"You sure you don't want something to eat? The cake here is really great." I cut a piece off with the fork and put it in my mouth.

"No, thanks," he says.

"Okay, so we're here. What did you want to talk about?" I put my fork down and pick up my coffee, blowing on it before taking a sip.

"What you said last night, at Grayson's place…about the real possibility of him getting jail time for the drug possession? Was that true?"

I put my cup down and lean back in my seat, staring at him. "Yes. Grayson isn't a drug user. The police took a look at the regular tests that athletes take. Grayson has taken these tests for the past twelve months, and since he's always showed up as clean, a hundred percent of the time, the police know the drugs weren't for personal use. And the amount he was carrying…well, even without the clean testing, they have enough evidence to pin an intent to distribute charge to him."

"I didn't know," Tyler says as he shakes his head, putting his cup down and staring into it.

"Grayson is hanging by the skin of his teeth onto the life he's living, and that's only because the press hasn't gotten wind of his arrest yet. The moment they do, his endorsements will go. He might still be allowed to play until his case goes to trial. But if he's found guilty, the team will drop him. And it wouldn't matter anyway, because if he goes to jail on the felony possession of the second degree charge, he'll be too old to go back into the pros when he's out, even if a team agrees to take him after he's damaged his reputation this much."

"I didn't realize."

"You knew how many drugs he had on him, and you had to know the police wouldn't think it was for personal use."

"But I thought with him being who he is…they'd just let it go."

I let out a dry laugh. "Police and judges love to make examples out of famous names—sports celebrities especially. With my old boss on the case, there was no way Grayson was getting off clean from the moment they found the drugs on him."

"But he said—"

"It was Grayson's idea."

He stares me in the eye. Then breaks contact and blows out a breath. "He won't be happy I'm telling you this."

"He'll be less happy if he ends up living in a prison cell."

"That night I was out with Grayson. I had that stash on me. I wasn't actually selling yet. I would never do that around Grayson. But I was out and he called me—asked me to come meet him for a drink. So I went along for one. I was planning to leave and hit up some clubs after, sell the shit on me."

"But the cops showed up?"

He nods. "I panicked and told Grayson I was carrying. I knew that if I got caught with the drugs, I was going down. Grayson told me to give them to him. That he wouldn't get searched because of who he is. I followed his orders. But then they searched him and carted him off." Tyler meets my stare and says, "I didn't mean for any of this to happen. And now I'm totally screwed. *We're* totally screwed."

"You're not screwed. All you have to do is tell the truth. I can help you."

"You don't understand," he says, picking up his coffee and taking a big drink of it. "It's gone further than that now." He meets my eyes again. "You were right about what you said last night, about my bosses…not being happy. Shit." Tyler covers his face with his hands.

"Calm down. Talk to me."

He drops his hands and stares at me. "I got involved with the wrong people. The drugs…they're cartel drugs. I've been dealing for the cartel."

"Holy shit." The words came out loud, so I adjust my voice down to a whisper. "You're working for the cartel?"

Tyler nods. "The drugs that were seized from Grayson were part of my second run for them. I was supposed to sell them and bring back the money. But then Grayson was arrested. I didn't want to ask him for the money to pay them on top of everything else. So, I…damnit. I stole some drugs from the stash, hoping they wouldn't notice, so I could sell those to pay them the money I owed them."

"You took drugs from the cartel and were planning to pay them back with that money you made off of stolen goods? What were you thinking?"

"Clearly I wasn't!" he snaps. "I panicked. And now those drugs are gone, too, and I don't have any money to pay them. And when I got home from Grayson's late last night…my place had been shot up. And there was a note pinned to my wall…a warning. They knew I'd been arrested. They're telling me to keep my mouth shut. I don't think they know about Grayson's arrest or the missing drugs yet, because if they did, then they wouldn't have shot up my place as a message. There would have been someone waiting there with a bullet for my head."

"I still can't believe that you're involved with the cartel," I say, putting my elbows on the table, driving my fingers into my hair. This feels way out of my league.

"What do I do, Melissa? How do I fix this?"

I lift my stare to Tyler. I can see how afraid he is when he says, "I don't want anything to happen to Grayson because of me."

"Let me think about it. I'll figure out what to do. But first I need to talk to your brother. He has to know what's been going on with you."

"No," he says.

"Yes. I have to tell him everything—about the cartel and what happened to you last night. I don't think it's a good idea if you're there when I tell him. I need to have Grayson thinking rationally, not trying to kill his little brother. Once I have him thinking straight, I'll bring him around to talk to you."

"What do I do while you do that?"

"Don't go back to your place. Just in case the cartel wises up and comes looking for you. Do you have anywhere to go that they don't know about?"

He shakes his head. "No."

I pull the keys to my apartment from my bag. "Go to my place. You'll be safe there." I give him my address. "Don't call or speak to anyone. I'll try to be as quick as I can with Grayson. Then I'll come home and we'll figure this out—the three of us. Don't worry."

I get up, hanging my bag on my shoulder.

As I walk past him, Tyler touches my shoulder. "Thanks—for everything."

"Don't thank me yet. Thank me when this is all over, when you and Grayson are safe."

Chapter 20

I ARRIVE AT the Bubble and have an easy time getting in to see Grayson. The security guy from last night is on reception today and he recognizes me and leads me straight through. I head out to the field, knowing that's where Grayson will be.

He's scrimmaging with his teammates, so I take a seat up in the stands. Watching him out on the field is really something special. He's magical out there. His teammates are great, but Grayson shines especially bright.

Once the scrimmage comes to an end, he sees me sitting up in the stands. I watch him move toward me, removing his helmet, so I start to make my way down the steps. "Hey," I say, stopping on the bottom rung.

"Hey," he says, holding his helmet in both his hands. He stares down at it. "I was going to call you."

"You were?"

"Yeah," he says, shifting the helmet into one hand and running the other hand through his wet hair. I know that he's just run around the field, but I can't stop imagining that I've made that hair sweaty in bed instead. "I was going to call you as soon as practice was over." He steps closer to me—so close I smell the sweat on him. It's a primal male scent and I can't get enough of it. It does funny things to my stomach and makes my legs feel weak.

"I'm sorry," he says in a low voice. Reaching out, he wraps his large hand around my wrist, drawing my eyes to it. "I was totally out of it last night."

I lift my eyes from where we're joined and stare at him and say, "You don't need to always be at your peak performance with me, Grayson."

He lets out a soft laugh and says, "Using sports terminology now, are we, lawyer?"

I laugh, shaking my head. But then I take the humor out of my voice. "I'm serious. I want to be with you, and that means being with you when you're acting like yourself. All the time."

His hands move down from my wrist, and he takes hold of my hand.

My eyes fix on his.

"I'm still sorry."

"I know you are," I reply softly. Then I slide my fingers between his.

I see the surprise in his eyes and then watch them soften. He curls his fingers around mine, gripping them tightly. "Let me take you home," he says. And I know he means to use his time alone with me well.

"We need to talk."

"I know," he replies. "We can do that at my place."

"I do mean talk, Grayson. That isn't code for sex."

"Talk," he says, laughing. "I got it."

"Seriously. It's going to be about things you probably won't like and you have to promise not to throw me out of your house again."

His brows push together. "I won't ever do that again. That was a terrible idea, and I don't make the same mistake twice."

"I'm glad to hear it."

"Let me take a quick shower first. Then we can get out of here. I'll drive us back to my place."

For all the times I've fought it, I know that I want Grayson more than ever right now. More than I've wanted anything in my life.

And I'm tired of fighting it. Fighting him. So I settle on letting him take the lead so we can see where we end up. But I pray that I didn't just make a terrible decision.

Chapter 21

I STEP INTO Grayson's house, remembering my visit there yesterday. That was the first and only time I had been here. And it didn't go so well. I'm hoping this one turns out better.

"Can I get you something to drink?" Grayson says. He takes off his jacket and hangs it on the coatrack in the hallway.

I remove my own and hang it up, putting my bag away with it. "Water would be good," I say, and follow behind him, my heels clicking on the wooden floor. I really should have taken them off at the door.

"You don't want something stronger?"

I'm standing with my hand against the wall, reaching down to remove my shoes. When I look up, I see Grayson's eyes slide down my body to the foot I just freed from my heels. Something that smolders like lust ignites in his eyes. And it sets off a heat inside of me. Swallowing, I place my first shoe down and then quickly remove the other.

"Water's fine." I don't think alcohol would be a good idea around him, especially if one look is already setting me on fire.

We have a big problem on our hands right now. And we have to address it first if we want Tyler to stay safe.

I head into the kitchen, where Grayson is already at the fridge. He pulls out two bottles of water, walks over to me, and hands me one.

"You're a lot smaller without your heels," he says, a hint of something like humor or sex in his voice—or both, I think. Without my shoes, he's towering over me and the feeling is thrilling.

"I'm normal-sized," I say with a grin. "You're just weirdly tall." Then I make the mistake of meeting his eyes.

The air crackles between us with lust so thick it fogs up my vision. All I can see is him.

"I, er…" I stumble back a step. Seeing the breakfast bar, I move over to it and prop myself up on a stool. Feeling flushed, I unscrew the cap on my bottle and take a long pull of water.

Grayson moves around to the other side of the breakfast bar. He puts his unopened water down on the countertop and curls his hands around the marble edge. I put my water bottle down and keep my eyes on it as I slowly screw the cap back on.

I know he's staring at me, but I'm nervous to meet his eyes again. The more I look into his eyes, the more I get caught in their hold. It's easier for us to control ourselves when there are other people around, but when it's just me and him…it's impossible.

And my willpower is weakening by the second.

"So…" he says, voice low and decadent.

"I saw Tyler earlier," I say, cutting through the tension. We need to focus on his brother. "He called and asked me if I would meet with him, so I did."

The silence is palpable. I risk a glance at him.

Grayson's jaw is tight. But he doesn't look angry, he just looks closed off. It's a look I've seen on him before. "And what did he have to say?"

I squeeze the bottle tightly. "He told me the truth—that the drugs found on you were actually his."

Grayson doesn't move or speak. But I see his grip on the counter tighten, his knuckles whitening.

"Why didn't you tell me?" I ask, looking him in the eyes unafraid, because I know sex is the last thing on his mind right now.

"Because he's my brother." He says this like it's a given. Like there isn't anything he wouldn't do for him.

Emotion overwhelms me. I find myself wondering, again, what it'd be like to have someone who cares about you so deeply that they would literally do anything for you—put their own ass on the line, risk going to jail for you, potentially lose everything—just like Grayson is doing for his brother. I find myself envious of Tyler in this moment.

"And he told me that he's…" I bite my lip. I'm actually nervous to tell him this part.

"What?" he asks. His tone is impatient, as is the look on his face.

"He's involved with the cartel. That's where the drugs came from. He's working for them."

Grayson doesn't speak but his eyes say it all.

"This is serious, Grayson," I say, my voice nearly a whisper. "You could lose everything—seriously, *everything*."

"You think I don't know that? Damnit!" he says, pushing off the counter and stalking away from me to the other side of the room. He slumps down in a chair at the large glass kitchen table. He puts his elbows on his knees and his head in his hands.

I hesitate for a moment before I go to him. I slip off the stool and I move over toward him, my bare feet padding on the wood. He doesn't look up as I get close. He stays there with his head in his hands.

I lift a hand to touch him, then pause, hesitating once again. With my hand hovering in the air, it feels like I'm touching him. Like I'm making the decision to erase that line between us. I stare down at him, my heart beating wildly.

Then I press my hand to his head. His hair is much softer than I was expecting. I slide my fingers through it.

He lifts his head and his dark-green eyes meet mine.

"We can fix this," I whisper.

"How?" he asks, and for the first time, he sounds vulnerable. And that's what cuts me wide open. He's finally allowing me in.

"I know people who can help…all you have to do is tell the truth—you and Tyler."

He lifts a hand and wraps his fingers around my wrist. His eyes drift down from me.

There's a beat before he lifts them back to me. "Okay," he says softly. "Do what you need to do, and I'll talk to whoever you need me to talk to, just…Tyler…"

"I'll make sure he's safe," I say quietly. Our eyes are locked. My thumping heart skips, beating erratically. "You'll have to let George Simpson go so I can represent you and Tyler. I should, um, make some calls…" My hand is still on his head, his fingers still wrapped around my wrist.

"Yeah," he says. But neither of us moves or looks away. "Look, Mel. I can't tell you how much I appreciate what you're doing. My brother means the world to me and now you—you've quit your job, you're sticking your neck out… you're an amazing person."

Then he stands and my hand trails away from his head. But he doesn't let go of my arm as my eyes follow his body as it rises. Suddenly, we're face to face.

My mouth feels dry. I wet my lips with my tongue.

It's right then that I see it in his eyes, the exact moment he makes the decision to consume me. He yanks me into his body, my chest heaving into his, and his mouth crashes directly onto mine, and he kisses me.

And, boy, does he kiss me.

Hands in my hair, tongue in my mouth, he kisses me. And it's hot as hell. My hands are gripping his huge arms for support and my legs feel like they're going out from under me.

God, the man can kiss.

He's kissing me like it's the only thing he needs—like I'm all he needs. There's no aphrodisiac like it. He presses into my hip and the feeling of how much I turn him on does all kinds of crazy things to me. I slide my hands up his arms and wind them around his neck. He makes a deep sound of pleasure into my mouth. It ripples through me, hardening my already erect nipples and teasing my clit like a featherlight touch of his fingers.

His hands leave my hair and slide down my back, grabbing my ass through my pencil skirt. His mouth leaves mine, and the sensation leaves me panting, and then he kisses down my neck, his teeth grazing my skin and making me shiver. "I want you so bad," he rasps against my skin.

I'm sure I mumble something incoherent back. All rational thought has left my mind and I'm a mess of hormones. But more than that—I'm his completely. In this moment, he can do whatever he wishes to me.

His fingers find the hem of my skirt and pull it up, over my hips. Then his hands are back on my ass and he's lifting me, then placing me down on the table.

He stares down into my eyes as his large hands cup my face. "I've never wanted anyone the way I want you, Mel. You make me crazy—seriously, it's unbelievable how it feels so good and so right when I'm with you. I can't even sleep because I'm always thinking about you."

"I…" I swallow. "I feel the same—and…I want you. I want

you, too." As I speak, I'm pretty sure my face is the color of a tomato because for some reason, I can barely get the words out. I might be falling for him.

His lips break into a smile that could dissolve the panties I'm wearing and his eyes darken with lust. Then his mouth crashes back down on mine, kissing me, taking greedy pulls on my tongue as he sucks it into his mouth.

Jesus, that feels good—amazing. He feels amazing. And I need more of him. All of him. Reaching my hands down, I fumble for the button on his jeans. I pop it, then slide the zipper down and slip my hand inside. I barely get my fingers inside his pants when he catches hold of my wrist, stopping me.

I blink up at him in surprise.

He lowers his forehead to mine, his breath gusting over my mouth as he speaks. "I want to make love to you in my bed. But if you touch me here, it's game over, Mel. I will take you right on this table."

Sweet baby Jesus.

"Maybe I want you to give it to me on the table," I say, hardly sounding like myself at all. I sound kind of…husky and sexy.

"Christ," he breathes, and I take it as an invitation. I slide my hand inside his jeans, and he doesn't stop me. My fingertips make contact with skin. The fact that he isn't wearing boxer shorts sends me over the edge.

Holy God.

I curl my fingers around his cock, gripping him.

"Shit," he hisses. His hand comes down so he can shove his jeans down to the floor. He wraps his big hand around mine and moves my hand up and down, so we're both driving him wild. And, damn, it's hot.

"That's it, harder—grip me harder."

I tighten my grip, giving him what he needs. His hand leaves mine, and I keep working him up and down. He wraps my hair around his hand, and then takes my mouth in a hot kiss.

The hottest, wettest, dirtiest kiss I have ever experienced in my life. The kind of kiss that could make a girl come. And honestly, with his tongue in my mouth and his cock in my hand, I feel like I could at any second.

His hand drops from my hair and pulls my silk shirt out from the confines of my skirt, kissing me all the while. He unfastens a couple of the buttons, and after he breaks away from my mouth, he pulls the shirt over my head.

His eyes drop to my breasts, which are still covered by my white, lacy La Perla bra.

Moving back from him, I take my hand out of his pants. I reach back and unfasten the clasp on my bra. Sliding the straps down my arms, I drop it on the table.

When I look back to Grayson, his eyes are on fire.

His large hands come up and cup my breasts, and he brushes his thumbs over my nipples, making me shiver. His lips lift at the corner and he bites down on that smile. Then he lowers his head, taking one of my nipples in his mouth.

He swirls his tongue around and in less than a moment, I'm squirming. His mouth feels exquisite.

"God, Grayson," I pant. I'm burning up, desperate for his touch. I push my hips forward, needing contact…needing him.

He must have read my body language, because he drops to his knees before me. With his hands curling into my skirt, he tugs it off me. I lift my hips. Skirt gone, he yanks my panties down, tosses them over his shoulder, pushes my thighs apart, and puts his mouth on me.

"Oh, my God!" My head drops and my hands press to the table as they try to grip the flat surface. "Grayson!" I cry.

There, on Grayson's kitchen table, I have my first orgasm from him. *God, don't let it be the last.* It explodes out of me in a toe-curling, mind-blowing release. I'm still trembling when he gets to his feet.

"Do you know how hot you are?" His voice is a rasp, exuding pure sex. I feel it shiver through me.

"I know how hot you make me," I whisper.

His eyes flare with need. Then, his hand goes down and wraps around his impossibly hard cock. "You make me crazy," he says, sliding his hand up and then down slowly. My eyes are fixed on his hand, riveted. "I'm going to show you exactly how crazy you make me."

He reaches his other hand into his back pocket and pulls out his wallet while he keeps working his hand up and down his shaft. He flips his wallet open and pulls out a condom.

After he rips open the packet with his teeth, he slowly rolls the condom on.

When his cock is sheathed, his eyes lift back to mine.

I tremble from the look in them.

He moves in between my legs and takes my face in his hands, kissing me deeply. His tongue slides over mine in a mind-blowing, drugging kiss. He breaks away from my lips, his eyes burning into mine, and drops his hands from my face to grab my hips.

He pulls me forward so my ass is perched on the edge of the table, and he slowly pushes himself inside me.

The feel of him sliding inside me so deep is like nothing I've ever felt before. And the look in his eyes…I feel like he's staring right into the very heart of me. The parts of me that I keep hidden from everyone else.

I feel exposed, vulnerable, but also…safe.

While he's inside me with his hips pressed against mine, his hands come back up to my face. Cupping it, he kisses me again. Gently this time.

He starts to move, slowly at first. I moan into his mouth, and that's when his control seems to snap. Our tempo instantly picks up. He's driving into me and the feeling is beyond incredible.

Grayson starts moving with an animalistic need. My hands are on his back, nails digging into his skin. The only sound is the rasp of our heavy breaths. No words are needed because our bodies are saying everything.

And mine is saying a lot. The second orgasm hits me and I'm crying out Grayson's name, my nails digging deeper into his back. My orgasm seems to set him off, because he yells out a string of expletives, my name mixed in among them, as he comes right after me.

With his forehead pressed against mine, he closes his eyes and his breath comes out labored.

"Jesus," he says. "That was amazing. You're amazing."

I slide my hands down his back. "I didn't do a lot. It was all you."

"But you're what I needed—all I need, Mel—it's you."

Then he brushes his lips over mine, kissing me softly. He pulls out of me carefully and takes the condom off. I can't keep the smile from my lips, because this gorgeous man…the hottest man I've ever met…he just told me that the only thing he needs is me.

"You're smiling," he says as he reaches me, moving back between my legs. He slides his hands around my waist.

"I am."

"I like when you smile."

Then he lifts me, and instinctively I wrap my legs around his waist and my arms around his neck. He starts walking through the kitchen.

"Where are we going?" I ask.

His smiling eyes meet mine. "To my bed, so I can make you smile some more."

Chapter 22

IT'S DARK OUT and Grayson has fallen asleep beside me. I take a moment to look at him. He looks relaxed and at peace. It's a look I've never seen on him before. Something pulls at my heart. I knew I had feelings for the man, but in this moment, I realize how strong those feelings are and have the potential to be.

But I have a lot to do—a man's life is on the line—so I quickly slip out of bed. After the week that Grayson's had, I know that he needs his sleep, so I move carefully. I don't want to wake him. More than anything, I want to stay here with him, but I need to go. I need to help him fix this mess that Tyler has gotten them into.

I look down at Grayson, tempted to kiss him before I leave, but I resist. I tiptoe out his bedroom and downstairs to retrieve my clothes. After I grab my cell from my bag, I go into the downstairs bathroom. I fire off a text to Tyler telling him that everything is okay and that he should stay put at my place. I have a few things to do and then I'll be home.

My phone beeps with Tyler's reply immediately: Cool. I've eaten the entire contents of your fridge—hope that was okay? ☺

Chuckling, I reply: No problem. I'll be in touch soon.

I climb into a cab and give the driver my address. I stare out of the window at Grayson's house as the cab pulls away. I can still smell him all over me. The scent of him sends memories from the night screaming through my brain. My body shivers from those thoughts and then aches to be back with that man.

Closing my eyes, I breathe through the moment. Then, I turn on my work brain and fish my cell out of my bag. It's late, but I'm sure the person I need to call will be awake. I search through my contacts until I find his number. I press Call and put the phone to my ear.

"Mel?"

"Hey, Matt," I say carefully, noting the surprise in his voice. I can't say I blame him for it, since I haven't called him in a long time.

"Are you okay?" he asks with genuine concern in his voice. It makes me feel like a jerk for all the times I've been standoff-ish to him and for using him now. But, like I said, a man's life is on the line.

"I'm fine…but I need your help."

"I'm looking over some reports at the coffee shop near my place, the one we always used to go to."

"I'll be there in five minutes," I say, and end the call. Then I ask the driver to take me to the new location.

Five minutes later, I'm walking into the shop. The scent of coffee sends my nerves into overdrive as soon as I push the door open. It feels weird to be here with Matt, but I push that aside, because I know I'm here for Grayson. He and Tyler need help, and Matt will be the one to provide it. He might be a pain in the ass at times, but he's a damn good cop.

I order my coffee and head to his table.

"Hey," I say, hanging my bag on the back of my chair.

"Just like old times, being here with you," he says with a smile, tipping his mug at me.

I don't chastise him for the comment, even though he knows better than to act like that's the reason I'm here. I don't want to get into a battle with him, especially since it's best if I stay on his good side right now.

"So, what can I do for you?"

I glance around and my eyes catch on a guy sitting over by the back, who's glued to his cell phone. I'm going to have to take my chances.

The barista brings the coffee over. I wait for her to leave before I start talking in a low voice. I tell Matt everything about Grayson's situation from start to finish—how he covered for his brother by holding the drugs, where those drugs came from, how Tyler was threatened by the cartel.

Matt doesn't say anything the whole time. He sits there and listens to me talk, taking it all in. When I'm done, I sit there staring at him, waiting for him to say something.

"Well, that's an absolute mess, Mel."

After everything I've just told him, that's what he says. And he is right. It's a huge disaster.

"I know, and that's why I need your help—Grayson and Tyler need your help. We're talking about the cartel here, Matt. The minute they find out those drugs are missing... Tyler's as good as dead. And Grayson..." I trail off, because I can't bring myself to say the words.

Matt blows out a breath. It's a resigned sound and I'm not sure what it means. "I have a contact in the DEA," he tells me. "I can call him, see what we can do to get them out of the mess they've got themselves in." He reaches for his cell, and I reach over and put my hand on his arm. He pauses, his eyes meeting mine.

"Thank you, Matt," I say earnestly. I move my hand away and into my lap.

"You don't have to thank me, Mel. You need help, and I'm there."

Chapter 23

IT'S LATE AFTERNOON and I'm heading back to my apartment. I spent most of the day with Matt at the police station, meeting his DEA contact, Paulo Dresden. We were mapping out a deal with him. Dresden is a short guy with a receding hairline who smells heavily of smoke and drinks way more coffee than I knew any one person could. He seems like a good guy and Matt trusts him. They went to the academy together.

Most importantly, Dresden has pulled together a good deal for Tyler—well, as good a deal as a person can get in these circumstances. Things won't be easy for him, since the DEA is proposing a plan that will turn his life upside down—he'll have to get a new identity and move into the Witness Protection Program.

Everything rests on Tyler agreeing to do this, and I would like to think that's a possibility, especially if he feels the same way about his brother as Grayson feels about him. I would hope he'd also do anything to keep him safe.

I walk toward my door, a little apprehensive about seeing

the guys. Grayson joined Tyler at my place after I called to tell him it'd take me a while to sort things out at the police station. I'm sure they're going a little stir-crazy. They've been hunkered down all day.

My stomach flips at the thought of seeing Grayson. Grayson, who drove me wild last night. I force deep, steadying breaths to calm myself.

He's just a man. One you've spent half the night getting hot and sweaty with, but still just a man.

I open the door and let myself in. My eyes connect with Grayson's instantly. Seeing someone for the first time after you've had sex with him is always nerve-racking, but I didn't expect to feel the way I do looking at Grayson right now. Like my whole world is centered around this one man.

But suddenly my world gets flipped again. There's nothing in Grayson's face or eyes. They're emotionless and cold. And I don't know if he's angry with me for leaving before he woke or just indifferent about what happened between us last night.

My heart sinks. Grayson said a lot of things last night— telling me how much he wanted me—but men generally say those kinds of things when they've got their cock deep inside you. It doesn't necessarily mean they want you forever.

I force a polite smile and gesture for them both to sit in the plushy couch in my living room. "Thanks for your patience," I say, dropping into a chair across from them. I look at Tyler as I speak because it just seems easier to do. Looking at Grayson right now would be like staring at the sun—it'd blind me. I can smell his cologne, teasing and taunting me. I take a breath and decide to just go straight into it. "I spent the last fourteen hours or so with Sergeant Daughtry—"

"The cop who arrested me?" Grayson demands. His words force me to look at him, and when I do, I swear to God I see jealousy burning in his eyes.

Why would he be jealous? Grayson isn't looking at me like he cares about me. And he doesn't know Matt is my ex, any-way…does he?

"Yes. I went to Sergeant Daughtry—Matt—because I trust him—"

Grayson snorts.

I ignore him and focus on Tyler, who is giving Grayson the side-eye. "I told Matt everything both of you told me. I thought it'd be easier to work with Matt on this, since he was the arresting officer in both of your cases. There's no reason to bring a third party in. Also, Matt has a contact in the DEA named Paulo Dresden. He called Dresden, brought him in, and the three of us hashed out a deal for you, Tyler."

"What's the deal?" Grayson asks.

I look at him. His expression is still blank.

"The deal is that both of you make a statement that says that Grayson had nothing to do with the drugs the police found on him that night in Liv. You tell them the only thing Grayson did was hide them for you, Tyler. Even though the police found the drugs on Grayson, Matt is willing to let the charge drop so long as"—I focus on Tyler, because this affects him the most—"you give up names of the main players in the cartel who you work for, and you testify against them—"

"No," Grayson says, cutting me off.

"Gray…" Tyler says his name in a gentle warning.

"No, Ty. You take this deal, you know what that means? If you testify in a trial, your life will be in danger. You—"

"It's already in danger," Tyler cuts him off. "The second I got involved with these people I was putting my life on the line. I got involved and now I have to face the consequences by myself. I can't let my big brother face them for me." Tyler turns to me and says, "I'll be protected, right? By the DEA?"

"Yes. Full protection. Then…" I bite my lip, pausing, because I can guess how Grayson will react to this piece of information. "After the trial, you'll go into witness protection and be given a new identity."

"Hell, no," Grayson says, getting off the couch. "Tyler, you're not going into witness protection. If you go, I'll never see you again."

Tyler gets to his feet, turning to Grayson. "I have to do this. There's no other choice."

"I'll take the rap on the drug charge," Grayson says, turning to me. I can see the panic in his eyes. "I'll go to jail. Call Daughtry, tell him that's the way it'll be."

"No," Tyler says in a firm voice. "I'm not letting you mess up your life for me. I should have never let you take those drugs from me in the first place. This is on me. I screwed up. You have a life and a great career—I saw how hard you worked, all your life, to get into the NFL. And now you have Mel. I won't have you lose that because of me."

He puts his hands on Grayson's upper arms, looking him in the face. His voice drops lower and turns more serious. "Even if I was selfish enough to let you do that, it won't make any difference anyway, Gray. The cartel knows I was arrested— they left me my first warning when they came to my apartment. Once they realize that there are charges against you that match mine and that I stole those drugs from their stash, they'll put everything together and I'll be as good as dead. You too, man. I won't let that happen."

Tyler swivels his head toward me and says, "This offer from the DEA is the best chance I have. Right?"

I see fear in his eyes and a desperate need for support, so I give it to him. I push up to my feet and say, "He's right, Grayson."

Grayson looks at me and I see the moment he accepts the plan. Hurt fills his eyes and defeat slumps his shoulders. He pulls his eyes from me and back to Tyler. He takes Tyler's face in his hands, looking him in the eye. "I'll be there for you the whole way. I won't let you down."

"I know, Gray. I know. You never have."

Then Grayson wraps his arms around his younger brother, and I turn away to look out the window and give them their moment. It also gives me the chance to discreetly wipe away the tear that decided to show up and escape from my eye.

I hear Tyler clear his throat. Then he says, "So what now?"

I turn back to the brothers. "Now we go see Matt Daughtry."

Chapter 24

THE THREE OF US go to the police station. Grayson and I go in first, so he can give Matt his statement about what happened the night he was arrested. Next, it's Tyler's turn to give his statement. Then Matt brings Grayson back in and tells him that the charges against him are officially dropped.

I've got to say, even though I knew it was coming, it's still a relief to hear. Matt tells Tyler that he should expect a call from Paulo Dresden within the hour, since the DEA agent will now be in charge of Tyler's case.

Since Tyler is advised not to go back to his apartment, we decide that he'll go to a safe house until the DEA gets in touch regarding the next step. That's when they'll collect the names of the key cartel players that they need, and then they can start making plans for their arrest.

Even though the cartel doesn't know that Tyler is talking to the police or the DEA, there's still a distinct possibility that they could find out about the missing drugs. Tyler's apartment is definitely a dangerous place for him to be right now.

Matt walks us all out. Tyler is up ahead, Grayson is glued to my side, and Matt is on my other side, at a slight distance from me. I'm starting to get the distinct impression that Grayson knows that Matt and I have a history.

Grayson's been off whenever he deals with Matt. I mean, I know the guy arrested Grayson once, but Matt has helped him today—and he's helped his brother. Grayson should be grateful for that. But his snide comments and attitude haven't shown that. When he made a crack about my "best friend Matt" to me, I cottoned on to the reason for his problem with the guy.

He was definitely jealous.

Superstar Grayson Knight was jealous of Matt Daughtry. All because of me.

I won't deny that I got a little thrill from knowing that the green-eyed monster was at work on Grayson. Some things just make a woman happy.

But Grayson's jealousy confuses me, because he's been so incommunicative ever since last night. Not that I've rushed to talk about things either, but I think that I've been cordial. It's strange that this morning and around Matt…well, I'm half-expecting Grayson to pee on me, so he can mark his territory.

I guess Grayson and I do need to talk about what happened between us. I'm worried about what last night was for him.…What if he was just chasing the unobtainable? Maybe I was something forbidden to him. Something he couldn't have. Now he's had that something—*me*—maybe the thrill has worn off and he's just not interested anymore.

Maybe the jealousy thing with Matt is more about male pride than anything else.

I guess the only way I'll know is if I talk to Grayson about it. Have a proper conversation with him. And I will talk to Grayson, once we've got Tyler settled at the safe house.

"Thank you for all of your help, Matt," I say, offering a smile and also my hand. Even though shaking Matt's hand seems too formal after everything he's done, I don't think hugging him would be the best idea with Grayson standing right beside me like some sort of animalistic predator. Who knows what he would do.

Matt stares down at my hand in his. A chuckle escapes him as he shakes his head. "Anytime, Mel. I told you earlier: You need help, you call me first."

"I know. Thanks again."

Matt is still holding my hand, even though he's stopped shaking it.

Grayson clears his throat. I take that as my cue to move. I ease my hand from Matt's, giving him one last smile of thanks before I leave. I walk through the door that Tyler is holding open. Grayson is on my heel, his hand possessively on my lower back.

His touch surprises me. It's the first time he's touched me since last night. The skin that his hand presses against feels like it's on fire. Even though there are layers of clothing between his hand and my back, I can still feel the heat of his fingertips.

I lift my eyes to him. The look in his face is heated with anger and lust. The combination is one hell of a sight, and my needs flare to life. My need for him.

I break eye contact so I can breathe. This isn't a moment we need to be having now. But it's one we need to have soon, if my libido has any say.

We've just hit the sidewalk when suddenly I hear the screech of tires. I look up and see a car moving down the street toward us. Panic stiffens my spine.

The car is a black Escalade with full blacked-out windows and no license plate. I feel completely paralyzed as I watch it. Those windows lower, almost as if in slow motion. I see the guns poke out from behind them.

Matt yells something.

Tyler turns and yells, "Get down!" His words hit my ears, but it sounds like I'm hearing them underwater.

Everything seems to slow right down, almost to a stop. I'm frozen and the guns are pointed in my direction.

I'm going to die.

Out of nowhere, someone grabs me and throws me to the ground. A large body lands on top of me, covering me, just as the earsplitting shots are fired.

All I can hear is the sound of screams and bullets spraying everywhere.

My eyes are closed and my heart thunders in my chest. I

have never felt fear like this in my life. It seems like the gun-shots go on forever.

The deafening noise stops as quickly as it started. My breath is caught in my throat and I'm afraid that a second spray is going to be aimed at us. But then I hear the distinct sound of tires screeching away.

They've gone.

I almost cry in relief.

There's only silence for a long second, as if someone has hit pause on the world around me.

Then the yelling begins as everything instantly comes back to life. Grayson's voice is loud and clear as he speaks to me. He keeps it surprisingly calm as he says, "I got you, baby. Are you okay?" He doesn't move his body off mine.

"Y-yeah, I'm fine," I say, my voice trembling. "They didn't"—I mentally check my body for pain, but there's nothing—"I'm okay. Are you—?"

"They didn't get me. I'm fine."

"Thank God." I breathe a sigh of relief. I couldn't bear it if anything had happened to him.

Grayson lifts himself up slightly but doesn't move off me completely. It's almost like he's afraid to leave me.

"Tyler?" I ask, my voice still trembling.

"He's fine."

I follow his line of sight to see Tyler sitting on the ground, looking completely shocked but physically okay. Matt is with him, and seems uninjured. He's checking over Tyler.

I shift, turning my face so I can look at Grayson. He looks fine, calm, but I see the fear and disbelief in his eyes. And I know how he feels, because I'm right there with him. I've realized, in this moment, how much he's come to mean to me. I knew I cared for him. Now I know how much.

Grayson's looking deeply into my eyes.

There's this moment where something intimate passes between us. He cups my cheek in his hand. "Mel, I—"

But he doesn't get to finish whatever he was going to say. Police officers come swarming out of the building, ready to help. The wail of an ambulance gets louder until the vehicle pulls up close to us, and paramedics jump out to check over our injuries. Whatever Grayson was going to say to me gets lost in the mire.

Chapter 25

THE CASE STARTED to move faster once the cartel tried to take Tyler out. A shooting in front of civilians at a police station is a much more serious crime than some warning shots fired in an empty home. I sat with Tyler and the DEA agents while he gave his statement to them. Then I checked over the written report with him before he signed.

Grayson was on the phone with his father in another room. I didn't want to bother him, so I waved good-bye and left. I needed to be home to take a moment to collect my thoughts in the safety of my apartment. I wanted to take a hot shower and wash the day off me. Then I had plans to curl up on my sofa and drink a large glass of wine.

Besides, I thought that Grayson would want to be with Tyler right now. Someone tried to kill his brother today, and I know how important Tyler is to him. Talking to me about what happened between us last night is probably the last thing Grayson wants to do right now.

I was shot at today.

It feels surreal. I can't even think about what would have happened if Tyler and Grayson hadn't reacted as quickly as they did. Especially Grayson…when he threw me to the ground and put himself on top of me like that…he saved my life. And I haven't even thanked him for it.

Suddenly, there's a knock at my front door. I freeze with my wineglass halfway to my lips. I carefully put it down on the coffee table and get to my feet. I secure the belt on my robe since I'm naked underneath. Taking a deep breath, I tuck my damp hair behind my ears and quietly pad across the wooden floors in my apartment.

I've just made it to the hall when there's another knock.

"Mel, it's Grayson."

My heart sputters to a stop.

He's here.

Moving quickly, I reach the front door, and after checking the peephole, I throw it open. His eyes lift to mine. He looks tired and his hair is messy, like he's been running his hands through it. But he looks hot. So very hot.

"What are you doing here?" I say, and I don't mean it to sound as harsh as it does, but it comes out that way because I'm surprised.

"I needed to see you. And I wanted to make sure that you were okay."

"I'm fine."

His gaze drops, and I realize that the belt on my robe has loosened a little when I rushed over, exposing my cleavage to him. Green eyes lift back to mine, causing shivers to break out all over my body.

The next thing I know, he's stormed through the door and slammed it behind him. Then I'm in his arms and his mouth is on mine.

"Grayson!" I gasp.

He swallows up his name with a kiss. Then he backs me up against the wall. His hands go to my thighs and he lifts me, putting himself between my legs. I wrap them around his waist and start kissing him back.

We're all tongues, teeth, and deep moans. There's nothing finessed about this kiss. This is happening out of pure need. Grayson's hand goes to his jeans. I hear his zipper pull down, and a condom package tear open. He stops kissing me. Lips still pressed to mine, he stares into my eyes, a question in them.

"Yes," I say, more a breath than a word.

In one movement, he thrusts his bare cock up inside me.

"Oh, my God!" I cry.

He starts making love to me there, against my hallway wall, while he's still fully dressed and I'm wearing only my robe. The feel of him inside me…it's amazing.

He starts to move, his pelvis hitting my clit each time he hits home, driving me wild.

"You saved my life," I pant between thrusts.

He pauses, staring into my eyes. "I did what anyone would have done."

"No," I say. "Not everyone would risk their own life to protect me."

"I would never let you get hurt, Mel. Never," he tells me, and I know he means it.

"Thank you," I whisper, brushing my lips over his. "Thank you so much."

Grayson captures my mouth again in a hot kiss, sucking my tongue into his mouth and making me moan. Then he starts moving again, driving into me harder with each thrust, making me crazy with desire.

My orgasm is quick, hitting me with a powerful force, and I scream out his name. He thrusts up inside me, once, twice, and then I feel him start to climax. He groans my name as he comes undone. We stay there, panting, trying to catch our breath. Grayson's face is pressed into my neck, his mouth soothing hot on my skin. My arms are wrapped tightly around him.

"I want you," he says softly. His lips brush over the skin of my neck as he speaks. He lifts his head and stares into my eyes. "Not just this—sex—but *you*."

"I want you, too," I say breathlessly.

"No—that's not what I'm trying to say. You told me that I should always be myself around you, that you want to be with every part of me. And that's what I want. I want more. I want something good and real with you, Mel. When I woke up this morning and you were gone, I…felt empty. And I've never felt that before. Then I realized the emptiness was there because you weren't." He cups my face with his big hand, threading his fingers into my hair. "I don't want to wake up like I did this morning, wondering where you are."

"I didn't want to leave like that either, but I had to help—"

"I know. And I'm thankful that you helped my brother. But now this is about you and me. And I like you."

"I like you, too. A lot. A whole lot," I say with a smile, and it reflects in his eyes as they light up.

"So, we're doing this—you and me?" he asks softly.

"A…relationship?"

"Yeah, Mel, I mean a relationship." He grins. "You and me together. I want you to be my girlfriend. And I'm not just saying that because I'm still inside you."

My smile widens as I giggle. "Oh, well, I'm glad to hear it. But—"

"But what?" he says, frowning.

"Well, we haven't even been on a date, Grayson—unless you count trips to the police station and getting shot at on the street corner as dates."

"Sounds like I better take you on a real one tomorrow, then. First thing in the morning, let's go out to breakfast. That can be date number one. Then lunch for date number two. Then dinner—"

"I get it," I say, laughing. "But how about right now, you take me to bed and screw me until it's time to take me out."

Smiling, he moves off the wall, carrying me with him as he starts walking down the hall. He presses a soft kiss to my lips, then whispers over them, "Take my girlfriend to bed and screw her all night? Yeah, I can definitely do that."

Epilogue

Six months later...

I HEAR A KNOCK at my office door, and then Grayson's beautiful head pops over the threshold. "You ready to go, babe?"

"Yeah," I say, and smile at him. "Let me just finish this article—it's about my case."

"It's in the news already?"

"Yup. I'm so glad that the world is seeing the great Benedict Cross, State Attorney, for the scum he really is."

And all because of me. After the DEA had set the wheels in motion for Tyler, I approached Internal Affairs to report Ben. I couldn't sit with what I had heard him saying on the phone and what he had been trying to do to Grayson. What if he was going to target other arrested athletes in the same way?

As it turned out, Internal Affairs had been looking into claims about an illegal gambling ring, packed with tons of high-powered people, but they'd never had anything concrete to go on before. I worked with them to help bring it down, and Ben is no longer the state attorney. He's facing charges.

Grayson, Tori, and Matt suggested I run for his position, but

I didn't want to. Instead, I've been busy setting up my own practice. After I'd met Grayson, I realized that I had my career goals set in the wrong place. Now I want something different. I don't want to be a big fish in a sea of sharks who are more worried about politics and publicity than justice. I want to be a big fish in my own little pond, helping out the little guys who wouldn't get help anywhere else. I'm happier than I have ever been.

Working on the other side as a defense attorney took a little getting used to, but it helps that I have the luxury of only defending clients I truly believe to be innocent. And Grayson has been such a huge help and support throughout the process. It was scary setting up my practice and going out there on my own, but slowly, my business is starting to build. Since my first case assisting Internal Affairs was such a big win, I'm hoping word of mouth will help me pull in a decent client base.

"I just got off the phone with Tyler," Grayson says as he walks into the room and leans against the wall.

"Oh, yeah?" I ask. After Tyler had left, Grayson told me that he had slipped him a phone so he could call him. They were breaking the rules about witness protection, but I didn't say anything about it. My boyfriend can't let his brother go completely, and I understand that.

"How's he doing?"

"Really well. He has a job and he's dating someone."

"That's awesome," I say, and I mean it. Those weekly check-in calls from Tyler are everything to Grayson. He doesn't know where Tyler is living, but that's for the best. I don't want anyone going after Grayson, and the cartel would if they thought he had information on his brother.

The trial itself was hard on everyone, but thankfully, some dangerous people were put in prison for a long time due to Tyler's testimony. He managed to make it through that stressful period without any more attempts made on his life. We had minimal contact with him in the run-up to the trial, and when it was over, Tyler went into witness protection right away. The whole thing has been very hard on Grayson.

I look up at him waiting for me. His smile lights up his face, giving me butterflies in my stomach.

God, he's so gorgeous.

Sometimes I still can't believe I'm dating *the* Grayson Knight. I never was one for the jocks in high school. But I didn't know what I was missing out on back then. Serious stamina and lots of muscle, and in this case, a beautiful heart and mind.

"Ready to go?" I ask him. And for the first time, I notice that he's being awfully quiet. Maybe a little jittery. "You wanted to grab dinner out, right?" I ask him.

"Sure. But first…" He pushes his hand into his pocket and pulls out a key.

"What's this?" I ask.

"A key to my place."

A smile breaks out on my face. "You're giving me a key to your place?"

"I am."

My smile gets wider. Walking over to him, I curl my hand around the key, taking it from him. "Wow. This feels like a big step. A great step, though. Thank you so much. Do you want a key to my place?"

"No," he says.

My smile drops. "No?"

He takes my hands in his. "I don't need a key to your place…because, well, I'm hoping that I already have one."

"Okay…" Confused, I furrow my brow.

"Babe…I'm not just giving you a key to my place. I'm asking you to move in with me."

Oh. Wow. An even bigger step than I expected.

"You want me to move in with you?" The words rush out of me, my heart quickening.

He smiles softly and says, "More than anything. Question is…do you want to move in with me?" I can hear the nerves clearly in his voice.

There's no hesitation in my answer. I part my lips and say, "More than anything."

His face breaks out into the biggest and most beautiful smile I've ever seen. "Good," he says, "because I love you and I think that we have something good going on here. And I can't wait to live with you to explore it." Then he kisses me, and it feels like a lifetime of kisses to come. Grayson leans his head back, staring down into my eyes, and asks, "So. Are you ready to go home?"

Smiling, I hold up the key he just gave me and say, "Our home? Can't wait."

About the Author

SAMANTHA TOWLE began her first novel in 2008 while on maternity leave. She completed the manuscript five months later and hasn't stopped writing since. She is the author of *The Mighty Storm, The Bringer,* and the Alexandra Jones series. She lives with her husband, Craig, in East Yorkshire, England, with their son and daughter.

Looking to Fall in Love in Just One Night?
Introducing BookShots Flames:

Original romances presented by James Patterson that fit into your busy life.

Featuring Love Stories by:

New York Times bestselling author Jen McLaughlin

New York Times bestselling author Samantha Towle

USA Today bestselling author Erin Knightley

Elizabeth Hayley

Jessica Linden

Codi Gary

Laurie Horowitz

…and many others!

Available only from

A PERFECT MATCH

Siobhan came to New York with a purpose: she wants to
become a successful artist. To pay her bills in the meantime,
she's the hostess at the Stone Room, a bar for the beautiful
and the billionaires. She's fine with being on her own—until
tech billionaire Derick takes her breath away.

**Read the first book in the Diamond Trilogy, *Dazzling*,
coming soon from**

HER SECOND CHANCE AT LOVE MIGHT BE TOO GOOD TO BE TRUE....

When Chelsea O'Kane escapes to her family's inn in Maine, all she's got are fresh bruises, a gun in her lap, and a desire to start anew. That's when she runs into her old flame, Jeremy Holland. As he helps her fix up the inn, they rediscover what they once loved about each other.

Until it seems too good to last…

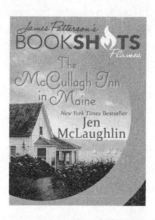

Read the stirring story of hope and redemption
The McCullagh Inn in Maine, **available now from**

SHE NEVER EXPECTED TO FALL IN LOVE WITH A COWBOY....

Rodeo king Tanner Callen isn't looking to be tied down anytime soon. When he sees Madeline Harper at a local honky-tonk— even though everything about her screams New York City—he brings out every trick in his playbook to take her home.

But soon he learns that he doesn't just want her for a night.

Instead, he hopes for forever.

Read the heartwarming new romance
Learning to Ride, **available now from**

THE MOST ELIGIBLE BACHELOR ON CAPITOL HILL HAS MET HIS MATCH.

Abbie Whitmore is good at her security job—until Congressman Jonathan Lassiter comes along. The presidential hopeful refuses to believe that he's in danger, even though Abbie's determined to keep him safe. But how can she protect him while she's guarding her own heart?

BODYGUARD

BY JESSICA LINDEN

READ THE SUSPENSEFUL ROMANCE, COMING SOON FROM

SOME GAMES AREN'T FOR CHILDREN....

After a nasty divorce, Christy Moore finds her escape in
Marty Hawking, who introduces her to all sorts of
experiences, including an explosive new game called
"Make-Believe."

But what begins as innocent fun soon turns dark, and as
Marty pushes the boundaries further and further, the game
just may end up deadly.

**Read the new jaw-dropping thriller *Let's Play
Make-Believe,* available now from**

BOOK**SHOTS**

"I'M NOT ON TRIAL. SAN FRANCISCO IS."

Drug cartel boss the Kingfisher has a reputation for being violent and merciless. And after he's finally caught, he's set to stand trial for his vicious crimes—until he begins unleashing chaos and terror upon the lawyers, jurors, and police associated with the case. The city is paralyzed, and Detective Lindsay Boxer is caught in the eye of the storm.

Will the Women's Murder Club make it out alive—or will a sudden courtroom snare ensure their last breaths?

**Read the new Women's Murder Club story,
available now only from**

BOOK**SHOTS**

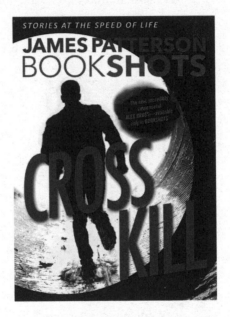